jB M877b
Blakely, Roger K.
Wolfgang Amadeus Mozart

The Importance Of

Wolfgang Amadeus Mozart

These and other titles are included in The Importance Of biography series:

Christopher Columbus
Marie Curie
Benjamin Franklin
Galileo Galilei
Thomas Jefferson
Chief Joseph
Michelangelo
Wolfgang Amadeus Mozart
Richard M. Nixon
Jackie Robinson
Margaret Sanger
H.G. Wells

THE IMPORTANCE OF

Wolfgang Amadeus Mozart

by
Roger K. Blakely

Lucent Books, P.O. Box 289011, San Diego, CA 92198-9011

Library of Congress Cataloging-in-Publication Data

Blakely, Roger K. (Roger Kellogg)
  Wolfgang Amadeus Mozart / by Roger K. Blakely.
    p. cm.—(The Importance of)
  Includes bibliographical references and index.
Summary: A biography of the composer from his days as a boy wonder to his adult success, his last years, and his death.
  ISBN 1-56006-028-X (acid-free paper)
  1. Mozart, Wolfgang Amadeus, 1756–1791—Juvenile literature. 2. Composers—Austria—Biography—Juvenile literature. [1. Mozart, Wolfgang Amadeus, 1756–1791. 2. Composers.] I. Title. II. Series.
ML3930.M9B62   1993
780'.92—dc20
[B]   92-41357
                                                          CIP
                                                         AC MN

Copyright 1993 by Lucent Books, Inc., P.O. Box 289011, San Diego, California, 92198-9011

No part of this book may be reproduced or used in any other form or by any other means, electrical, mechanical, or otherwise, including, but not limited to photocopy, recording, or any information storage and retrieval system, without prior written permission from the publisher.

Contents

Foreword	7
Important Dates in the Life and Times of Wolfgang Amadeus Mozart	8

INTRODUCTION
In Search of Mozart — 11

CHAPTER 1
Boy Wonder — 17

CHAPTER 2
Toward Self-Knowledge — 27

CHAPTER 3
A Changed Life in Changing Times — 38

CHAPTER 4
Boom Times — 52

CHAPTER 5
Good Luck and Bad — 64

CHAPTER 6
The Last Years — 74

CHAPTER 7
Who Murdered Mozart? — 84

CHAPTER 8
Mozart Then and Now — 94

Notes	101
Glossary	103
For Further Reading	106
Works Consulted	107
Index	109
Picture Credits	111
Acknowledgments	111
About the Author	112

Foreword

THE IMPORTANCE OF biography series deals with individuals who have made a unique contribution to history. The editors of the series have deliberately chosen to cast a wide net and include people from all fields of endeavor. Individuals from politics, music, art, literature, philosophy, science, sports, and religion are all represented. In addition, the editors did not restrict the series to individuals whose accomplishments have helped change the course of history. Of necessity, this criterion would have eliminated many whose contribution was great, though limited. Charles Darwin, for example, was responsible for radically altering the scientific view of the natural history of the world. His achievements continue to impact the study of science today. Others, such as Chief Joseph of the Nez Percé, played a pivotal role in the history of their own people. While Joseph's influence does not extend much beyond the Nez Percé, his nonviolent resistance to white expansion and his continuing role in protecting his tribe and his homeland remain an inspiration to all.

These biographies are more than factual chronicles. Each volume attempts to emphasize an individual's contributions both in his or her own time and for posterity. For example, the voyages of Christopher Columbus opened the way to European colonization of the New World. Unquestionably, his encounter with the New World brought monumental changes to both Europe and the Americas in his day. Today, however, the broader impact of Columbus's voyages is being critically scrutinized. *Christopher Columbus,* as well as every biography in The Importance Of series, includes and evaluates the most recent scholarship available on each subject.

Each author includes a wide variety of primary and secondary source quotations to document and substantiate his or her work. All quotes are footnoted to show readers exactly how and where biographers derive their information, as well as provide stepping stones to further research. These quotations enliven the text by giving readers eyewitness views of the life and times of each individual covered in The Importance Of series.

Finally, each volume is enhanced by photographs, bibliographies, chronologies, and comprehensive indexes. For both the casual reader and the student engaged in research, The Importance Of biographies will be a fascinating adventure into the lives of people who have helped shape humanity's past, present, and will continue to shape its future.

Important Dates in the Life and Times of Wolfgang Amadeus Mozart

Death of J. S. Bach.	1750	
	1751	Birth of sister Maria Anna (Nannerl) Mozart.
Birth of Wolfgang Amadeus Mozart, January 27.	1756	
	1762	Plays before Empress Maria Theresa.
First composition for piano.	1763	
	1763–1766	Tour to Paris and London with father and sister.
Birth of Beethoven.	1770	
	1769–1771	First Italian tour: opera *Mitradate* in Milan.
Second Italian tour: opera *Ascanio in Alba* in Milan	1771–1772	
	1772	Colloredo becomes Salzburg ruler.
Third Italian tour: opera *Lucio Silla* in Milan.	1772–1773	
Visits Mannheim and Paris. Mother dies.	1776	United States declares independence.
	1777–1779	Joseph II succeeds Maria Theresa.
Premiere of opera *Idomeneo* in Munich; final quarrel with Colloredo; settles in Vienna.	1780	
	1781	Schiller's protest play, *The Robbers*.

Premiere of opera *The Abduction from the Seraglio* in Vienna. Marriage to Constanza Weber.	1782	
	1784	Beaumarchais's *Marriage of Figaro*.
Years of the great piano concertos; completion of "Haydn" quartets; *Marriage of Figaro* in 1786.	1785 1786 1787	Death of Leopold Mozart. *Don Giovanni* produced in Prague. Appointed court composer at low salary.
Composes last three symphonies. Financial difficulties.	1788 1789	American Constitution framed. French Revolution begins.
Tours the German cities of Berlin, Dresden, Leipzig.	1790	
Premiere of operas *The Clemency of Titus* in Prague and *The Magic Flute* in Vienna. Mozart dies December 5, leaving the *Requiem* unfinished.	1791	Premiere of opera *Cosi fan Tutte*. Journeys to Frankfurt for coronation of Leopold II. Death of Joseph II.
	1798	Wordsworth and Coleridge stimulate British romanticism.
Napoleon becomes virtual dictator of France.	1799	
	1805	Beethoven's *Eroica* Symphony.
Goethe's *Faust*, Part One.	1808	
Constanza Weber Mozart remarries (Georg Nissen, Danish diplomat).	1809	Death of Haydn.
	1815	Napoleon defeated at Waterloo.

IMPORTANT DATES IN THE LIFE AND TIMES OF WOLFGANG AMADEUS MOZART

Introduction

In Search of Mozart

The 1991 bicentennial of Mozart's death on December 5, 1791, generated many new books, articles, and other information about this great musician. Even earlier, in the 1980s, the film *Amadeus* sparked popular interest by telling how the villainous rival Salieri hastened the young genius's death because of his envy of a far greater talent.

But much of this information is of doubtful accuracy, and some of it is downright wrong. For example, the middle name Amadeus, or "God-beloved," made popular by the movie was almost never used by the man himself. Mozart preferred the French version, Amadée, or no middle name at all. And this is only one of dozens of innocent or perhaps deliberate errors forced on the public by popular treatment of Mozart, whose personality was so unusual and yet so human that he still mystifies the world. In fact, even men and women of his own day found his music and his character baffling.

In spite of a legendary skill at mental composition, Mozart did not create every piece of music in his head and then write it down while playing pool. Though his speed, accuracy, and inventiveness as a composer were phenomenal even at a young age, some major works, by his own admission, needed preliminary drafts and corrections. In fact, his own statements on this matter are contradictory. Of his string quartets dedicated to Franz Joseph Haydn, he wrote in 1783 that they "are, indeed, the fruit of a long and laborious study."[1] Yet, a few years earlier, a letter to his father

An idealized and very unreliable portrait of Mozart as an adult, painted after his death.

In this idealized painting, Mozart gives an impromptu concert.

describes his method for putting together parts of the full-length opera *Idomeneo* before its premier in Munich: "Well, I must close, for I must now write at breakneck speed. Everything has been composed, but not yet written down."[2]

Evidently his method changed, depending on the task at hand. And far from being pressured constantly by the need to compose, Mozart produced music not only or chiefly for his own pleasure, but to earn money. Of course there is nothing crass or shocking about supporting one's self and one's family. Practical motives cannot tarnish the splendor of the G Minor Symphony or the opera *Don Giovanni*. Both of these masterworks sound as fresh now as in the years of their origin. Yet we should view Mozart on everyday terms as a workman and a professional who worried about finances and careers just as we do. This attitude makes him seem more approachable without diminishing the power of his music.

Was Mozart a freak with an IQ of 250, a large skull, and a withered body, as some biographers imply, or just another ordinary mortal with a highly specialized skill? The question invites both simple-minded answers and fanciful ones. It is true that such creative intellectuals as Shakespeare, Newton, Darwin, and Emily Dickinson seem different not only in *degree* but also in *kind* from the rest of us; yet their roots lie in common humanity. Otherwise they would be freaks, indeed, and their doings and sayings would not reach out to others. We would lump them instead among those idiot savants who compute square and cube roots without pencil and paper or spout every ballplayer's batting average from Honus Wagner to the present. It is important that, in spite of his particular talent, Mozart had his share

The only known surviving ticket to a Mozart concert in Vienna during the 1780s.

> ## A Friend Remembers Good Times
>
> *The Irish tenor Michael Kelly sang in the premiere of Mozart's* The Marriage of Figaro. *In this quote taken from Otto Eric Deutsch's book,* Mozart: A Documentary Biography, *Kelly describes Mozart as he knew him.*
>
> "Madame Mozart told me, that great as his genius was, he was an enthusiast in dancing, and often said that his taste lay in that art, rather than in music. He was a remarkably small man, very thin and pale, with a profusion of fine fair hair, of which he was rather vain. He gave me a cordial invitation to his house, of which I availed myself, and passed a great part of my time there. He always received me with kindness and hospitality. —He was remarkably fond of punch, of which beverage I have seen him take copious draughts. He was also fond of billiards, and had an excellent billiard table in his house. Many and many a game have I played with him, but always came off second best."

and more of ordinariness. Without this quality he could not have created the intensely human scores of *The Marriage of Figaro* or *The Magic Flute*—a pair of operas full of idealism, bombast, meanness, beauty, love, and all the stops along the full scale of our emotions.

Not only was Mozart's music tuned to the concerns of his era, but his intellectual and spiritual life was, too. He was both an orthodox believer who wrote church music and a child of the Enlightenment—that epoch of reason and brotherhood that helped to spark the American and French revolutions and put an end to the divine right of kings.

Mozart experienced mundane worries and enjoyments throughout his life. He enjoyed mild obscenities—and some raw ones. Word games and riddles amused him, and occasionally he wrote semiserious poetry, such as the elegy for a pet bird that begins like this:

> A little fool lies here
> Whom I hold dear—
> A starling in the prime
> Of his brief time,
> Whose doom it was to drain
> Death's bitter pain.[3]

He partied happily with Viennese cronies. Like many other parents, he fretted that his son's boarding school expenses cost more than the quality of its instruction warranted. He scolded his wife for alleged loose behavior, though he was sometimes guilty of the same. He hit up acquaintances for loans and behaved with equal generosity when *he* had money. He sometimes gambled. Certainly he liked games, though witnesses disagreed over his abilities. One of his letters mentions composing a piece while bowling—probably the Italian boccie. At one time he actually owned and rode a horse. Whether he was a skillful rider or a novice remains unrecorded.

Acquaintances remarked on his friendliness and sense of humor. He was described as five-foot-four, pale, with protuberant eyes and a large nose. He was always alert and even jumpy, rattling keys or fiddling with napkins. A long apprenticeship as a public performer that dated from early childhood removed any traces of stage fright. He performed on keyboard instruments or violin and viola with equal skill. Mozart's ability at the organ brought an offer of the organist's job for the royal chapel at Versailles—a position he refused in spite of its prestige because of the low pay.

He taught piano students, wrote lessons for them, proposed—but unfortunately never carried out—a treatise on music fundamentals, and wrote perhaps the best series of letters by any musician at any time. Some of these concern serious matters; others reveal the frivolous and even vulgar side of a chameleonlike personality.

Young Mozart also conceived harebrained schemes that drove his father up the wall. Perhaps the worst was a proposed concert tour with his new friend, the singer Aloysia Weber, and her papa—members of a family of unreliable Bohemian artists in his own father's opinion.

Along with his native German, Mozart spoke and wrote French and Italian fluently, knew a smattering of English, and of course understood the church Latin of religious texts.

Mozart as an Intellectual

These glimpses of a lively and versatile Mozart are part of the record, but not the whole of it. Neither the superman of some legends nor the giggly childlike man of the film *Amadeus,* he thought deeply, if intermittently, about cultural and philosophical issues. Even as a job-hunting youngster in Paris, he wrote home to his father, Leopold, about asking "God daily that He grant me to strive for the greater honor of our entire German nation."[4]

Having Fun

In a letter translated and quoted by Emily Anderson, the composer describes playing word games during a journey to Prague in 1787.

"Now farewell, dearest friend, dearest Hinkiti Honky. That is your name, so that you know. We all invented names for ourselves on the journey. Here they are. I am Punkititi. My wife is Schabla Pumfa. Hofer is Roozka-Rumpa. Stadler is Natschibinitschibi. My servant Joseph is Sagadarata. My dog Gauckerl is Schamanuzky."

Germany was not yet an organized nation, but a smorgasbord of duchies, monarchies, and other units that included Prussia, Austria, Bavaria, and—at least in theory—parts of the old Holy Roman Empire. Thus Mozart must have had in mind German culture as a whole, or what we would nowadays call a Germanic ethos.

Mozart's philosophical side is revealed in a famous letter mailed from Vienna to his ailing father in Salzburg on April 4, 1787, only a few months before the older man's death. It was meant to comfort Leopold and at the same time to state the son's own views on the subject of death. When Wolfgang's own turn came three years later, he looked death in the face with similar frankness.

> As death, when we come to consider it closely, is the true goal of our existence, I have formed during the last few years such close relations with this best and truest friend of mankind, that his image is not only no longer terrifying to me, but is indeed very soothing and consoling. And I thank God for graciously granting me the opportunity (you know what I mean) of learning that death is the key which unlocks the door to our true happiness. I never lie down at night without reflecting that—young as I am—I may not live to see another day. Yet no one of all my acquaintances could say that in company I am morose or disgruntled.[5]

The cryptic aside, "you know what I mean," must refer to the stoic teachings of Freemasonry, a semisecret organization that both father and son had joined. To balance his masses and other church works, Mozart wrote equally profound music honoring this new "faith" that had evolved into a fraternal society for the more liberal nobles and laymen who were committed to the new ideals of Reason and Benevolence.

What Mozart himself could not accomplish, even with the support of these two

Detail from an unsigned painting of a secret Masonic meeting in 1790. The person seated at far right is Mozart.

"religions,"—Catholicism and Freemasonry—was to live past his thirty-fifth year. This fact shrouds his active, many-faceted, almost bumptious career in an atmosphere of sorrow and even tragedy as we look back from a two-hundred-year perspective. But Mozart could not know this doom, even though he was psychologically ready for it, and he lived fully, creatively, and usually optimistically, except during financial crises. During the last two weeks of his deathbed struggle, all of his bodily functions seemed to break down at once. At the end, rheumatic fever, heart trouble, kidney failure (or whatever else modern medicine determines from long-ago evidence) finished his short, spectacular career.

Mozart Today

When tracing this man's brief, controversial history, we should remember that his music is truly everlasting. Tapes and recordings abound. Thousands and tens of thousands of piano students have practiced Mozart sonatas, while professional soloists make a growth industry of his concertos. Some tunes even show up in TV commercials. His operas are staged worldwide in either period or modern dress, and lately in ghetto or African-American versions. The classical form for symphonies and other large-scale compositions as developed by Mozart and his friend Haydn dominated the music of the nineteenth century. Only his *Requiem* seems exalted enough to accompany the funerals of heads of state.

Even as we read these lines, someone is performing Mozart—either expertly, or horribly off-key, but in hopes of eventual improvement. Of his sonatas for pupils, it has been said that some are too easy for amateurs and too hard for highly skilled virtuosos. This suggests, probably, that no one can exhaust the possibilities of the sonatas. Even such later giants as Ludwig van Beethoven and Richard Wagner called Mozart their master. Beethoven, true heir to Mozart, performed in one of the first concerts given to aid Mozart's widow Constanza, in Vienna in the mid-1790s, at the start of a similarly fabulous career.

How music that seems so inevitable, so melodic, so truthful to our own feelings could have poured forth in such quantity and quality from a man who lasted only half a lifetime—well, that's the puzzle confronting us. Though dying abruptly and only half-appreciated by contemporaries, Mozart left more than six hundred compositions. Among them are forty-one symphonies, twenty-seven piano concertos, and operas of three hours' duration or longer, scored for a half-dozen solo voices, chorus, and full orchestra. All his works show painstaking craftsmanship and an effortless flow of melody. And this vocal and instrumental output was accomplished by hand, before computers, photocopiers, and other gadgetry eased a composer's physical burden.

On at least one occasion Mozart scored a full operatic overture the night before its first performance. The ink was hardly dry when his orchestra had to play it. As a boy, and after a single hearing, he copied out a motet that had been performed in the Vatican without ever seeing the written music. Maybe there is a supernatural side to this very human man after all!

Chapter 1

Boy Wonder

The birth of a prodigy often surprises us because the parents of such exceptional people may be quite ordinary or only slightly above average. Also, even a genius needs the good luck of parental and societal encouragement, good instruction, and sufficient emotional and physical stamina to weather the conflicts a talented individual suffers under even the best conditions.

Such was the situation in 1756 for Wolfgang Mozart, the last of seven children (only he and a sister survived infancy) born to Leopold Mozart, a capable but not remarkably gifted court musician to the prince-archbishop of Salzburg. This tiny but independent city-state lay at the foot of the Alps in western Austria, more than 150 miles from much larger Vienna, the capital of a great empire.

Leopold had received a good education in Augsburg and Salzburg before abandoning any thought of the priesthood and leaving the university to pursue his real love, music. As violinist, teacher, and author of an important treatise on the art of violin playing, he became known throughout Europe. He was a broadly cultured gentleman, perhaps considered superior to most of the people around him and therefore restless in his circumstances, but able to tolerate them—especially after the birth of his wunderkind, or child prodigy, son.

Wolfgang's mother, Maria Anna Pertl, was witty and industrious, though not well educated. His older sister Maria Anna, nicknamed Nannerl, also showed early musical talent but never turned this talent into a major career. Except as singers, women were not then encouraged or accepted by society

Wolfgang's mother, Maria Anna (née Pertl) Mozart, painted by an unknown artist in 1775.

A fanciful picture, done long after the composer's death, shows a three-year-old Wolfgang trying to play his father's clavier.

as professional musicians. While her brother was achieving international fame, Nannerl stayed home and taught piano and later married an elderly, minor nobleman in nearby St. Gilgen. Early in his own career Wolfgang wrote piano pieces for her. If Nannerl did some composing of her own, as some researchers maintain, none of it survived.

Wolfgang's fortunes, however, flourished from the start. At the age of three he had discovered pleasing combinations of notes and at five actually wrote a concerto. Though this scrawl was scarcely legible, his father found it playable after careful study. Much later, Johann Schachtner, a family friend, recalled the incident in a letter to Nannerl that expressed adult astonishment at the small boy's feat:

> His father took [the manuscript] from him and showed me a smudge of notes, most of which were written over inkblots which he had rubbed out.... At

Wolfgang's sister, Maria Anna, nicknamed Nannerl, at age twelve.

Playing the Violin Without Lessons

Otto Eric Deutsch's Mozart: A Documentary Biography *records the surprise of Johann Schachtner, a family friend, upon hearing a seven-year-old play the violin:*

"Wolfgang had asked to be allowed to play the second violin, but Papa refused him this foolish request, because he had not yet had the least instruction in the violin, and Papa thought that he could not possibly play anything. Wolfgang said: You don't need to have studied in order to play second violin, and when Papa insisted that he should go away and not bother us any more, Wolfgang began to weep bitterly and stamped off with his little violin. I asked them to let him play with me; Papa eventually said: Play with Herr Schachtner, but so softly that we can't hear you, or you will have to go; and so it was. Wolfgang played with me; I soon noticed with astonishment that I was quite superfluous. I quietly put my violin down, and looked at your Papa; tears of wonder and comfort ran down his cheeks at this scene, and so he played all six trios. When we had finished, Wolfgang was emboldened by our applause to maintain that he could play the first violin too. For a joke we made the experiment, and we almost died for laughter when he played this [part] too, though with nothing but wrong and irregular positioning, in such way that he never actually broke down."

---

first we laughed . . . but his father then began to observe the most important matter, the notes and music; he stared long at the sheet, and then tears, tears of joy and wonder, fell from his eyes. Look Herr Schachtner, [he] said, see how correctly and properly it is all written, only it can't be used, for it is so very difficult that no one could play it. [Wolfgangerl] said: "That's why it's a concerto, you must practice it till you get it right, look, that's how it goes." He played, and managed to get just enough out of it for us to see what he intended.[6]

Young Mozart's progress on the violin was equally remarkable. Besides a thorough coaching in all branches of music, father Leopold drilled him in languages and mathematics. Such an education may have been spotty, but not unduly narrow by the standards of those times.

Barnstorming

For various reasons—money, improved social status, and a wish to hasten the development of both children—the father applied

The Mozart family about 1780, by the painter J.N. della Croce. The mother, who had died two years earlier, is represented in the oval wall portrait—a common practice among painters at the time.

to the archbishop for leave from his own position to take them on tour in 1762. After a brief stay in Mannheim, a city full of good musicians, he brought Wolfgang and Nannerl to sophisticated Vienna. By the time he was six, the little prodigy's fame resulted in an invitation to play before the Austrian queen-empress Maria Theresa and her court. According to stories that soon circulated, Wolfgang jumped into the lap of this most powerful woman in Europe to give her a kiss. Of course a cuddly child in silken tunic, knee britches, and powdered wig could dare anything; and at this tender age, he even proposed to Princess Marie Antoinette, suggesting they marry when both of them were older. In hindsight, such a match may or may not have boosted a musician's career, but it might have saved an unlucky future French queen from the guillotine.

In spite of Wolfgang's various childhood fevers and other illnesses, the father staged a much longer tour for the whole family, from June 1763 to November 1766. The itinerary led them through what is now southern Germany, where they stopped for performances along the way and enjoyed the luxury of their own carriage, rather than the uncomfortable public stagecoaches of that era. Their goal was Paris, where the children's fame had preceded them and resulted in appearances at court and an audience with King Louis XV. Wolfgang tried the sumptuous chapel organ at Versailles, home of French kings for several generations. Quite an exploit for a seven-year-old!

Wolfgang in gala costume at age seven. Fine clothes such as these were worn for recitals or when meeting royalty and nobility.

In her memoirs of 1800, ten years after Wolfgang's death, Nannerl charmingly described her brother as traveling companion in their junkets across Europe:

> Mozart's over-rich imagination was so lively and so vivid, even in childhood, at a time when it still lies dormant in ordinary men . . . that one cannot imagine anything more extraordinary and in some respect more moving than its enthusiastic creations; which, because the little man still knew so little of the real world, were as far removed from it as the heavens themselves. Just one illustration: As the journeys which we used to make (he and I, his sister) took him to different lands, he would think out a kingdom for himself as we traveled from one place to another, and this he called Das Königreich Rücken—the Kingdom of Back—why, by this name, I can no longer recall. This kingdom and

At the keyboard (far left) young Wolfgang entertains Prince Conti's stylish guests in Paris. The event is depicted by M.B. Olliver in this 1776 painting.

its inhabitants were endowed with everything that could make good and happy children of them. He was the King of this land—and this notion became so rooted within him, and he carried it so far, that our servant, who could draw a little, had to make a chart of it, and he would dictate the names of the cities, market towns and villages to him.[7]

It's true that other bright children such as the Brontë girls and their brother invented fantasy lands inhabited by lords, ladies, fairies, and villains. Today science fiction fills the same role for modern readers of all ages. But in Mozart's case the Kingdom of Back returned as the realm of Sarastro, high priest of the composer's last and most profound opera, *The Magic Flute*.

The Mozarts liked England well enough to spend more than a year there. During this time Wolfgang played before King George III, staged successful public concerts, and studied under Johann Christian Bach, youngest of Johann Sebastian's several brilliant sons and the leading composer of his adopted country. On their return home through the Netherlands, brother and sister fell dangerously ill from typhus, a disease spread by lice and marked by high fever, rash, and sometimes delirium (confusion and hallucinations). Many die from the disease, so it is surprising that Nannerl and Wolfgang survived, given the backwardness of medicine and indifference to sanitation in the late 1700s.

Exposure to popular music in Paris and London stimulated the boy wonder to

A view of London at the time of the Mozart family's visit in the 1760s shows the Westminster Bridge in the foreground.

compose his first symphony. Upon the family's return to Salzburg, the skeptical archbishop Schrattenbach, normally a lenient ruler, evidently doubted this young man's prowess: he locked Wolfgang in a room and challenged him to write a choral number within two hours. When finished—and on time—it proved good enough for church performance along with the works of mature composers.

Mozart showed a keen ability to notice and absorb the musical styles around him and then to go them one better. In this transitional period from baroque to classical, the learned counterpoint (interweaving of melodic lines according to strict rules) gave way to the looser rococo mode. The latter style emphasized emotion and decoration, often with an accompaniment that was simple and easy to comprehend. In turn, the mid-1700s style of Bach's sons and the Mannheim composers evolved into the versatile but tightly structured music of Haydn, the later Mozart, and their great follower Beethoven. Thus, even at a tender age Mozart stood on the threshold of new things while still solidly grounded in past methods: an ideal formula for artistic breakthrough.

The Lure of Italy

By the age of ten Mozart had performed for three crowned heads of Europe and had given many public performances, often to rave reviews. But as the faddish popularity of a child wonder yielded to adolescence, and Nannerl grew well beyond the prodigy stage, Leopold's tactics altered. Indeed, the father has been criticized for exploiting his son's talents, robbing the boy of a normal child-

Leopold, Wolfgang, and Nannerl as they might have appeared on tour, painted by Louis Carrogis de Carmontelle in 1764 or 1765.

hood, drilling him in harmony, counterpoint, instrumental methods, and music literature (along with liberal arts subjects) until the poor child dropped from exhaustion.

Such notions degrade both of them. Wolfgang was an eager learner, his father a skilled educator. More importantly, Leopold knew that in order to enter the musical life of Europe, a sheltered lad from Salzburg must see more of the world. Wolfgang would have to rub shoulders with masters of his craft and learn all the varieties of musical styles he must employ as a professional.

Both father and son acknowledged the challenges ahead. The art of composition would become Wolfgang's field of study,

A Fussy Father

W. J. Turner, in Mozart: the Man and His Works, *cites an unfavorable view of the elder Mozart.*

"It is interesting to note that Hasse [a prominent composer of opera] wrote on March 23, 1771, to the Abbé Orres: 'The young Mozart is certainly a marvel for his age and truly I love him boundlessly. The father, as far as I can see, is eternally discontented with everything . . . he idolizes his son a little too much and so does all he can to spoil him, but I have such a high opinion of the natural sense of the boy that in spite of his father's flattery I expect him not to let himself be spoiled but to grow into a proper man.'"

Portrait of Leopold Mozart in 1765 by an anonymous artist. Although Mozart and his father often disagreed, the two remained close.

A Student to His Teacher

In a letter of September 4, 1776, to Padre Martini of Bologna, one of his early teachers, Mozart seeks his former mentor's approval. The excerpt is taken from Emily Anderson, The Letters of Mozart and His Family.

"We live in this world in order to learn industriously and, by interchanging our ideas, to enlighten one another and thus endeavour to promote the sciences and the fine arts. Oh, how often have I longed to be near you, most Reverend Father, so that I might be able to talk to and have discussion with you. For I live in a country where music leads a struggling existence, though indeed apart from those who have left us, we still have excellent teachers and particularly composers of great wisdom, learning and taste. As for the theatre, we are in a bad way for lack of singers. . . . If we were together, I should have so many things to tell you! I send my devoted remembrances to all the members of the Accademia Filarmonica. I long to win your favour and I never cease to grieve that I am far away from that one person in the world whom I love, revere and esteem most of all."

and Italy—the center of European music since the Renaissance—his university. The next few years allowed father and son to make three trips across the Alps, thanks in part to leaves of absence for Leopold provided by that same kindly archbishop, for the senior Mozart was now assistant *kapellmeister*, or music director, of the court orchestra.

Of course Wolfgang still performed the trained monkey role of his childhood when required, and evidently without complaining. Perhaps "the smell of the greasepaint and roar of the crowd" so dear to all entertainers enticed him. Yet his own interests leaned more toward creating, rather than re-creating, music. Lessons with the famous counterpoint teacher Padre Martini of Bologna, election to the musical academy of that city after passing its tests in record time, and a visit to Naples followed his youthful performances.

From Naples, father and son poked about the volcano Vesuvius like ordinary tourists. In Rome the Vatican bestowed on Wolfgang the Order of the Golden Spur—a rare tribute that the much older and more famous composer Gluck had to wait half a lifetime to obtain. Composing and conducting the grand opera *Mitradate* in Milan at age fourteen climaxed these successes for Wolfgang. *Mitradate*, commissioned by the state theater, paid him one hundred ducats (an equivalent of nearly ten thousand dollars today—a ducat was worth about ninety dollars), plus free lodging and a cast of excellent singers. Quite a stroke of luck for a fourteen-year-old!

Mozart at age twenty-one proudly wears the Order of the Golden Spur award, given to him by the pope several years earlier.

Many letters home charted the journey of father and son through Italy. In a chatty mood, Wolfgang practiced Italian in a message to Nannerl. In German he added praise for a harmony exercise she had sent him for corrections. Always sensitive to *sound,* he asked about "Mr. Canary. . . .Does he still sing? And still whistle? Do you know what makes me think of him? Because there is a canary in our front room which makes a noise just like ours."[8]

This letter and others show that an adolescent's unusual intellectual growth during his midteens had not obscured a sense of fun or a love of ordinary family matters. In less than a year Leopold and Wolfgang would set forth on a second Italian tour, with still more to be learned.

Chapter 2
Toward Self-Knowledge

In the years from 1771 to 1779, Mozart grew rapidly as both musician and mature human being. Several operettas for Austrian audiences and the grand opera *Mitradate* in Milan had already given the boyish composer experience in theatrical writing and its customs. Opera was as widespread in popularity then as rock-and-roll is now, though aimed at a somewhat different audience, but it was becoming pompous and artificial. Leading composers were the German Johann Hasse; Niccolò Jommelli; the well traveled Bohemian master Christoph Willibald Gluck; and later, Mozart's competitor Antonio Salieri, and his friend Giovanni Paisiello, whose flair for comedy paved the way for *The Marriage of Figaro*. Most of them wrote too much, and without originality.

Opera seria, or "grand opera," suffered from ironclad rules. Soloists made big news, like rock stars do today. Their arias (solos) commonly required *da capo* (from the beginning) repeats of the first sections with added vocal fireworks, while other cast members stood idle and audiences in the private boxes gossiped, since they already knew or had guessed the plots. In between arias came tedious recitatives, narrative sung in speechlike rhythms to meager accompaniment from the harpsichord or orchestral instruments.

Ballets sometimes stopped what little action there was in these operas; the chorus had not fully evolved into a participant in the drama; duets or larger ensembles seldom broke the monotony. Most of the score was formulaic (unimaginative), tied to a few harmonic progressions and cadences—almost prefabricated. Only a major talent

Portrait of a young man with a diamond ring (1771) identified by some scholars as Mozart. Its authenticity is very doubtful.

such as Handel's, thanks to the vigor and variety of his tunes, could surmount such obstacles, and he had died in 1759.

The plots were no better. Material from classical sources dominated. Over and over again the stories of Dido and Aeneas, the Trojan War, Greek gods and goddesses, or events from Roman history appeared. Mozart's early operas could not escape this dead hand from the past. The kingpin of the tradition, Pietro Metastasio, wrote twenty-seven librettos from which a host of composers drew some eight hundred musical settings. Whether or not audiences grasped its nuances, or subtleties, Italian was the preferred language for opera in most countries. Only later would comedic plays by the Italian Carlo Goldoni *(The Liar, The Servant of Two Masters)* or Frenchman Pierre-Augustin Beaumarchais (the Figaro plots) lighten this heavy fare, along with a native German-language *singspiel,* a form that mixed spoken dialogue with folktunes.

Christoph Willibald Gluck, forty years Mozart's senior and in due time his admirer, was smart enough to urge needed reforms. He believed that music should adjust to the action, rather than obey artificial formulas. Instead of that stale da capo scheme, let arias express genuine emotions in a natural manner, rather than become excuses for trills and runs and high Cs. Recitatives might benefit from richer accompaniment, and powerful overtures should prepare listeners for the coming events. And—a distinctive Gluck contribution—the chorus could set moods or comment on action as in the old Greek tragedies of Sophocles and other dramatists.

Mozart was not yet ready for all of these improvements. He was, however, excited by a return engagement in Milan,

Christoph Willibald Gluck was a prominent opera composer and an important influence on Mozart's artistic development.

Italy—this time a commission from Maria Theresa herself, the empress into whose lap he had bounced as a child. His task was to write a *serenata theatrale* as part of the marriage ceremonies for a member of the royal family. Leopold called the composition a "short opera," but *Ascanio in Alba* more nearly resembled a tableau of shepherds, nymphs, dancers, and a stage wedding blessed by Venus. Evidently Wolfgang intended that using this character to symbolize the Austrian ruler would be flattering to her.

It sounds stagey and obsolete. In fact, modern audiences cannot take these early Mozart operas seriously. He was not yet skilled enough, nor free enough, to revolutionize made-to-order music. But he liked *Ascanio,* and it enjoyed several performances after the official premiere. Perhaps some of its songs could still succeed in concert form. On the whole, however, the reviewer of a modern revival at a 1960s Salzburg Festival saw the weaknesses:

> Mozart caused an entirely natural sensation with his early works. In many of them—and by no means in all of those that were written for the mass requirements of contemporary courts—there is even a distant rumbling of his future genius. But it is impossible to turn back the clock, except for study purposes in seminars. Once the public has discovered the mature genius, it will no longer be interested in the "previously future genius," unless the boy has left behind works that are still of interest in themselves. This is all that matters in the theater. And who, apart from the arranger Bernhard Paumgartner, could ... tolerate this *Ascanio* on any stage if this tentative experiment on the part of a 15 year old were not listed in Köchel [the directory of Mozart's pieces]? To present it nowadays ... is tantamount to pronouncing a death sentence on almost everyone concerned.[9]

At any rate, Mozart's assimilation into Italian culture was incomplete. Whether flash in the pan or future grand master, he longed for good, old-fashioned home cooking. As his father wrote to the family back in Salzburg, Wolfgang once asked for—and enjoyed—"liver dumplings and sauerkraut" as the guest of a transplanted German family.[10]

A third and last trip south, in the winter of 1772 and 1773, also yielded an opera, *Lucio Silla,* that paid the composer well and was performed twenty times. It disappeared from nineteenth century repertoires, however, and was not published in complete form until the 1880s. Modern

A violin part from the orchestral accompaniment to an aria in Mozart's Lucio Silla.

> ### An Antique Plot
>
> W. J. Turner's Mozart: the Man and His Works *neatly summarizes the action of* Lucia Silla, *a typical grand opera.*
>
> "The plot is as follows: Silla [the Roman Sulla] loves Giunia, promised bride of the Senator Cecilio, and determines to kill Cecilio after vainly having represented him as dead in order to win over Giunia. The lovers decide to die together. Silla then pardons them and gives his sister Celia in marriage to Cecilio's friend, Cinna, renounces the dictatorship, and gives Rome back her freedom."

music lovers will know it only from the one or two flashy soprano arias that are occasionally performed on the concert stage.

Of these attempts in a stodgy, archaic (antiquated) style, only *Mitradate* has been revived successfully in America recently. In spite of many negative opinions, the current verdict on young Mozart is: not all bad, and in places fairly good as a token of better things to come. But he would learn to slough off the ragged garments of grand opera. The violence and intrigue of its bad characters and the self-righteous stuffiness of the good guys resulted in melodrama rather than in true accounts of human emotions. Gradually he would learn how to capture such emotions without frills and tricks. By 1786, the time of the performance of *The Marriage of Figaro,* he had brought opera up to date with the changing social and political times.

But in the mid-1770s such quantum leaps in creativity would have to wait. Back in Salzburg, the city seemed more provincial than ever under the rule of a new taskmaster, Prince-Archbishop Colloredo. A

Salzburg's ruler and Mozart's boss, the Prince-Archbishop Colloredo. Mozart was the concertmaster of Colloredo's small orchestra.

maturing composer must have longed to flee, just as gifted young people nowadays prefer New York City to Cedar Rapids, Iowa, or Amarillo, Texas. Yet he slaved away as the newly appointed concertmaster (conductor and first violin) of Colloredo's small orchestra and also as cathedral organist.

He found some time to compose, and the religious piece for soprano, "Exultate Jubilate," became the earliest Mozart work still regularly performed. It is an elaborate three-movement concertolike piece for voice and orchestra, easily on a par with the true concertos for violin from the same era.

Still learning his craft, he also wrote several modest piano concertos that often adapted ideas from other composers: string quartets, divertimenti and other incidental music, and a number of symphonies. More advanced works such as the first major piano concerto (in E-flat, K. 271) showed greater command over both orchestration and musical structure. (K. 271 is a cataloging designation for a composition. See the glossary for further explanation.) The opening back and forth between soloist and group in K. 271 (rather than the customary tutti, or full ensemble introduction for orchestra alone) became a musical declaration of independence.

Paris Again

Mozart felt ready for a larger and more appreciative audience than Salzburg provided. Colloredo actually suggested that the young man should return to Italy to learn more about music. Then this autocrat rejected Leopold's application for a leave to take his son to Paris in search of better opportunities. Since both parents considered Wolfgang too young and flighty to visit France alone, poor Frau Mozart, who disliked journeys, was dispatched as chaperone for this fateful adventure.

Letters back and forth between father and son let us follow the next few months closely. In more than one of these, Wolfgang expressed growing contempt for the archbishop. From Paris the gripes continue. Occasionally he turned from personal grievances to shrewd commentary on the war in Bohemia and on British-French fighting that was a spinoff from their rivalry in North America. A later note from Munich labeled Colloredo the chief villain. Only on his father's account would Wolfgang continue to work for such a rascal. "If I had followed my inclination," he goes on, "I would have wiped my behind with my last contract."

Strong language indeed—and it was not so much the citizens of Salzburg "but the Prince and his conceited nobility who become every day more intolerable to me."[11] So strong were his sentiments, in fact, that Mozart wrote part of this communication in code to evade Colloredo's spies and censors.

But immediate escape was foiled by Mozart's inability to find good prospects in Paris. His friends' efforts to interest the

> ## The Trouble with Salzburg
>
> *Emily Anderson's* Letters of Mozart and His Family *quotes a letter written on August 7, 1778, from Paris to Wolfgang's Salzburg friend concerning his growing dislike for his native city:*
>
> "You, most beloved friend, are well aware how I detest Salzburg—and not only on account of the injustices which my dear father and I have endured there, which would be enough to make us wish to forget such a place and blot it out of our memory for ever! But let us set that aside, if only we can arrange things so as to be able to live there respectably.... Perhaps you will misunderstand me and think that Salzburg is too small for me? If so, you are greatly mistaken. I have already given some of my reasons to my father. In the meantime, content yourself with this one, that Salzburg is no place for my talent. In the first place, professional musicians there are not held in much consideration; and secondly, one hears nothing, there is no theatre, no opera; and even if they really wanted one, who is there to sing? For the last five or six years the Salzburg orchestra has always been rich in what is useless and superfluous, but very poor in what is necessary."

French authorities came to nothing. Worst of all, his mother sickened and died on July 3, 1778, of an undiagnosed fever—lonely, far from home, and unable to help or oversee her son's affairs. Wolfgang found it difficult to break the news to his father, and he delayed almost a week. On July 9, 1778, he finally informed Leopold, as gently as possible:

> I hope that you are now prepared to hear with fortitude one of the saddest and most painful stories; indeed my last letter of the 3rd will have told you that no good news could be hoped for. On that very same day, the 3rd, at twenty-one minutes past ten at night my mother fell asleep peacefully in the Lord; indeed, when I wrote to you, she was already enjoying the blessings of Heaven—for all was then over. I wrote to you during that night and I hope that you and my dear sister will forgive me for this slight but very necessary deception; for as I judged from my own grief and sorrow what yours would be, I could not indeed bring myself suddenly to shock you with this dreadful news! But I hope that you have now summoned up courage to hear the worst, and that after you have at first given way to natural, and only too well justified tears and anguish, you will eventually resign yourself to the will of God.[12]

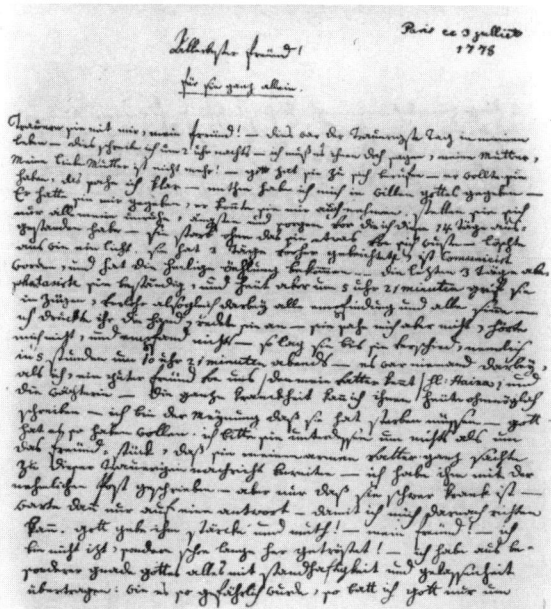

In this letter dated July 3, 1778, Mozart writes from Paris to family friend Joseph Bullinger in Salzburg.

Thus Paris was personally tragic as well as professionally disappointing, aside from several performances and the creation of a fine symphony geared to French tastes. Mozart's return to Salzburg must have been the low point in his life so far. Even so, he produced in the *Coronation Mass* of 1779 his most stalwart church music to date, carefully tailored to Colloredo's demand for brevity and simplified ritual.

This was the consequence of a general program of austerity in Salzburg's parishes under their new leader. Actually, except for his treatment of Mozart, Colloredo was a progressive and energetic prelate (high-ranking clergyman) who would go down in history with a better reputation. Though the musical world remembers him as the bully who kicked a great composer downstairs, scholars tell us that it was not Colloredo but one of his courtiers who did the deed—and not until two years later, when relations between employer and employee broke down forever.

Music or Romance?

The expedition to and from Paris had brought other complications. Of course Mozart felt the emotional and social pressures of an adolescent as well as an ambition for worldly success. The city of Mannheim, his stopover en route to France and back again, supplied a new circle of performers and composers to the Salzburg court's orchestra, perhaps the best and most up to date in Europe. It was known for excellent woodwinds, precision timing, and a bold use of crescendo and decrescendo (increasing, and decreasing, volume). These qualities, along with brisk melodies on top of a nervous and rather simple 4/4 rhythm, popularized the "Mannheim sound."

Mozart was influenced by this sound, as can be heard in *Sinfonia Concertante* for violin and viola (K. 364) of 1779. His vice of compulsively repeating four- or eight-bar measures that sometimes bores us works beautifully here. The violin's soprano sound and the smooth, liquid contralto of its partner, the viola, constantly toss musical phrases back and forth. Hugh Ottaway, an enthusiastic modern critic, calls this splendid work "one of the first Mozartian masterpieces of indisputable genius. In the outer movements, seriousness and lightness are reconciled; with their sprightly use of oboes and horns, these movements have much of the atmosphere of Salzburg serenades, but also a spaciousness and depth."[13]

Concert hall of the National Theater in Mannheim, a musical center Mozart visited in the mid-1770s. Mozart was greatly influenced by the wonderful musicians in Mannheim and wrote several pieces with them in mind.

But the impact of Mannheim's culture had not monopolized this young man's attention. Among his new friends were the conductor Cannabich, at whose house Mozart's latest compositions were played and sung, and this man's lively fourteen-year-old daughter Rosa, for whose keyboard lessons Mozart wrote a sonata. No doubt he flirted a bit, too.

More troublesome was his acquaintance with a copyist of scores and a musical jack-of-all-trades Fridolin Weber and the man's four daughters, destined to play important roles in Mozart's later life. Of these girls, Aloysia, the second oldest, seemed greatly talented and attractive. Even before completing the trip to Paris with his mother, and perhaps with a nudge from Herr Weber, a bewitched Mozart talked of touring Italy with these folks. Aloysia's fine voice would be featured, and money would be made.

Upon learning of these plans, Leopold's alarm back in Salzburg is easy to understand. After all, he had not spent so many years grooming a prodigy only to run afoul of charlatans (those with more showmanship than skill). Mozart's mother, more and more helpless as a watchdog, added her warnings to the son's trial balloon:

MY DEAR HUSBAND.... You will have seen from [Wolfgang's] letter that when Wolfgang makes new acquaintances, he immediately wants to give his life and property for them.

True, [Aloysia Weber] sings exceedingly well; still, we must not lose sight of our own interests. I never liked his being in the company of Wendling and Ramm [other Mannheim musicians], but I never ventured to raise my objections, nor would he ever have listened to me.

But as soon as he got to know the Webers, he immediately changed his mind. In short, he prefers other people to me, for I remonstrate with him about this and that, and about things which I do not like; and he objects to this. So you yourself will have to think over what ought to be done. . . . I am writing this quite secretly while he is at dinner, and I shall close, for I do not want to be caught. Addio. I remain your faithful wife, MARIA ANNA MOZART.[14]

Mozart's sister-in-law, soprano Aloysia Lange in a typical opera costume of the period.

Parents of a youth today who runs around with motorcycle gangs or chooses the wrong girlfriend will sympathize. As for poor Frau Mozart, we know that she did indeed continue to Paris with her rebellious son, only to die there. And as for Leopold, of course he tackled the emergency quickly. His return letter to Wolfgang of February 11–12, 1778, filled several pages and mentioned his son's great future—*if* present temptations were overcome:

> And now it depends on you alone to raise yourself gradually to a position of eminence, such as no musician has ever attained. You owe that to the extraordinary talents which you have received from a beneficent God; and now it depends solely on your good sense and your way of life whether you die as an ordinary musician, utterly forgotten by the world, or as a famous Kapellmeister, of whom posterity will read,—whether, captured by some woman, you die bedded on straw in an attic full of starving children, or whether, after a Christian life spent in contentment, honour and renown, you leave this world with your family well provided for and your name respected by all.[15]

Leopold's warnings seem less exaggerated when we remember that his son fell head over heels in love just a few years later—and not with the brilliant Aloysia, but with her plainer sister Constanza.

But that lay ahead, and the Italian adventure was wisely called off. For now, Wolfgang also dallied—mostly by mail, and not in earnest—with his cousin Maria Anna Thekla Mozart, nicknamed Bäsle, whom he had met while passing through

An Improper Correspondence

This excerpt from one of Wolfgang's letters to his Augsburg cousin Bäsle, is taken from Emily Anderson's Letters of Mozart and His Family. *The English translation reflects the original rhymes:*

"Why, of course I'm sure of success,
even if today I should make a mess,
though to Paris I go in a fortnight or less.
So if you want to send a reply to me
from that town of Augsburg yonder, you see,
then write at once, the sooner the better,
so that I may be sure to receive your letter,
or else if I'm gone I'll have the bad luck,
instead of a letter to get some muck.
Muck!—Muck!—Ah, muck! Sweet word! Muck! chuck!
That too is fine. Muck, chuck!—muck!—suck—
o charmante! Muck! suck!"

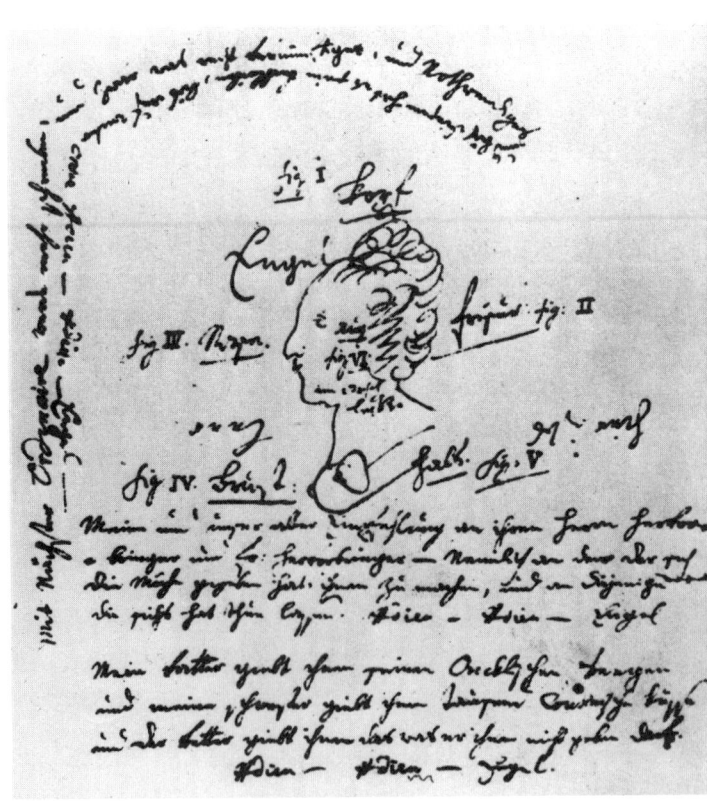

Manuscript, letter, and sketch from Mozart to his cousin Maria Anna (nicknamed Bäsle), dated May 10, 1779.

Unfinished portrait of Mozart, presumably at the piano, by his brother-in-law Joseph Lange. It is said to be the best likeness of the adult composer.

Augsburg. He liked her gaiety and physical attractiveness, and her mischievousness matched his own.

How mischievous? Well, enough to enjoy vulgar letters as private jokes between them, full of references to toilet functions. Their literary merit hardly matches the notes students of a certain age now pass back and forth in school. Not very elegant for a young man of Wolfgang's renown! But standards of behavior differed in the century of *Tristram Shandy* and Voltaire and other disturbers of the peace. Also, Mozart much later played word games of this sort with close friends and with his wife.

At the close of these crazy months, including the stay in Paris, Mozart's return to his hometown marked the end of a phase of his life. His failure at finding a permanent position and the loss of his mother were combined with loss of a sweetheart. This calamity occurred when Aloysia Weber, launched on her own career, spurned her musical admirer and married the painter-actor Joseph Lange—no doubt to Leopold Mozart's immense relief.

Chapter 3
A Changed Life in Changing Times

The next decade in Mozart's life, 1780 to 1790, was marked by rapid social change in Austria-Hungary. The quest of Haydn, Mozart, and others for personal and artistic freedom mirrored a restlessness throughout Europe's developed nations. America's struggle for independence and democracy cheered liberals as much as it terrified the old order, especially French and English conservatives. Reason, scientific experiments such as Benjamin Franklin's, and agitation for human rights threatened the political and cultural status quo.

Emergent middle classes resented the power and land ownership of the aristocracy. The rise of industry, better communications, and prospering cities made life somewhat easier, at least for the economically secure. As always, luxuries were monopolized by wealthy and privileged folks, but the number of these people grew. Feudal lords like the filthy-rich Esterhazys, possibly the wealthiest in Austria-Hungary, still maintained orchestras and in-house opera. Within more limited means, the merchants and lesser nobility copied their superiors.

The Esterhazy's house-musician Haydn won the right to travel abroad in the 1790s, and his two concert series in England brought him fortune and fame. Luigi Boccherini, Christoph Gluck, and others also established multinational reputations. Mozart, as we saw, left Salzburg at greater risk. Beethoven kowtowed to nobody: if great snobs offered to subsidize him, fine, but he would not take orders, nor even doff his hat to them.

Franz Josef Haydn (1732–1809) was Austria's leading musical figure and Mozart's faithful friend and supporter.

The reigns of Maria Theresa and her son who succeeded her, Joseph II, reflected some of the turmoil going on everywhere. Either jointly with a do-nothing husband or in her own right, Maria Theresa ruled Austria and its dependencies from 1740 to 1780. She picked good advisers, for example, Prince Kaunitz in foreign affairs, and Baron van Swieten—later a Mozart supporter—as director of education and other intellectual matters. If rivalry with Prussia and other powers occupied her at first, the relative peace of later years encouraged limited social reforms.

Beyond her flair for politics, Maria Theresa expressed some interest in the arts and even sang as an amateur in private palace theatricals. She was also a devoted but sometimes overpowering mother. The child Mozart amused her, though he lost some of his aura as an adult. A hard-nosed letter of 1771 to her younger son Ferdinand, then ruling Milan, disapproved of these Mozarts as candidates for official employment. She seems to have distrusted musicians in general, and German musicians particularly.

Joseph II was Austria's emperor from 1780 until his death in 1790. In spite of their many disagreements, Joseph remained Mozart's patron throughout his reign.

An Empress's Taste in Music

Edward Crankshaw's Maria Theresa *quotes from a letter to the empress's son Ferdinand in 1772 concerning the musical situation in Austria:*

"But for the theatre I confess that I prefer the least of the Italians to all our composers, whether Gassmann, Salieri, Gluck or anyone else. Now and then these produced a good piece, but when it comes to the ensemble, then I always prefer the Italians. For instrumental music there is a certain Haydn, who has some peculiar ideas, but he is only beginning."

You ask me about taking into your service the young Salzburger. I can't think what as, for I do not believe you have any need for a composer.... But if it would give you pleasure, I shall not prevent you. What I say is, do not burden yourself with useless persons, and the claims of such persons on your service . . . and [Leopold] has, further, a large family.¹⁶

Her attitude seems odd, since she had once expressed concern when the boy Wolfgang and his sister had fallen ill of smallpox (fortunately not severe) on an early visit to Vienna. She had also approved Mozart's writing of *Mitradate* for Ferdinand, and had moreover just staged Mozart's highly regarded wedding-piece *Ascanio*.

Truly, as the young composer learned over and over again, it would be tough to keep in favor with empresses, archdukes, and courtiers.

The Sorrows of Joseph II

Mozart's prospects improved after Maria Theresa died in 1780 and her son, Joseph II, became sole ruler of Austria-Hungary. History has been unkind to this man who was hardly kind to himself as a mixture of old-hat totalitarianism, or absolute authority, and Enlightenment liberalism. He attempted to abolish serfdom, opposed death penalties, confiscated monastic lands, and extended freedom of worship to non-Catholics. His militarism alienated followers, however, and he disliked criticism. His more radical or hasty decisions disturbed many of his subjects, whatever their own political leanings.

At first championing or at least tolerating Masons (Freemasons) and freethinkers, he began to fear their ties to revolutionary trends in France, where his sister Marie Antoinette shared the throne. Though posing as a friend of the common man and walking among his subjects without a uniform or armed guards, he did little to curb pomp and intrigue in the royal palaces. Ailing from tuberculosis, he became ill during a foolish war against the Turks and died after barely a decade on the throne.

His connections with Mozart were fairly close. Besides sponsoring *The Abduction from*

Mozart plays before Joseph II and his courtiers in this painting by a late nineteenth-century artist. Two noblemen behind the emperor obviously belong to an anti-Mozart clique.

> **Music Must Always Please**
>
> *Wolfgang's letter to his father Leopold of September 26, 1781, describes his effort, in composing the* Abduction, *to write descriptive music that will not sacrifice artistic values. This quotation comes from Emily Anderson's* Letters of Mozart and His Family:
>
> "As Osmin's rage gradually increases, there comes . . . the allegro assai [very fast section], which is in a totally different metre and in a different key; this is bound to be very effective. For just as a man in such a towering rage oversteps all the bounds of order, moderation and propriety and completely forgets himself, so must the music too forget itself. But since passions, whether violent or not, must never be expressed to the point of exciting disgust, and as music, even in the most terrible situations, must never offend the ear, but must please the listener, or in other words must never cease to be *music,* so I have not chosen a key foreign to F (in which the aria is written) but one related to it."

the *Seraglio* (Harem) as part of his German opera campaign, Joseph supported the Salzburg refugee in other ways, including providing performances at court and other commissions. On the other hand, he never provided a secure, well paying post such as Salieri and other favorites enjoyed. And after his death, an economy-minded brother, Leopold II, curtailed entertainments and shut the door on further reforms.

Despite the portrayal in the movie *Amadeus* of him as a crowned dunce who butchered the keyboard and fell asleep at concerts, Joseph was no fool. He was, in fact, a competent hobbyist musician, able to appreciate at least some of Mozart's brilliance. His private and state papers reveal an articulate but very conflicted personality. A letter to his first wife's father after her death expressed deep emotions:

I have lost everything. My adored wife, the object of all my tenderness, is gone. You have known my love for her and now will be smitten by the same misery as I. . . . Judge of my situation! Agonised and beaten down, I hardly know if I am still alive.[17]

His advisors urged a second marriage for reasons of state. This new spouse happened to be a smallpox victim whom he detested openly: "My wife has become unsupportable to me. . . . They want me to have children. How can one have them? If I could put the tip of my finger on the tiniest part of her body which is not covered with pimples, I would try to have a child."[18]

From this situation, a growing misogyny, or hatred of women, tainted Joseph's last years and possibly figured in his suggesting the plot of *Cosi fan Tutte* to Mozart—a lovely opera on the whole, but unflattering toward women.

Joseph also had some stubborn ideas that he forced on the people, including his insistence on clamping down on such funeral luxuries as fancy coffins and monuments. Instead, he favored simple interment in a body bag. So many citizens objected to this callous policy that he finally gave up the fight. The Masons also disliked showy funerals, and Mozart's speedy, controversial burial in an unmarked grave in 1791 may have reflected Joseph's continued influence even after the emperor's own demise.

The Battle of Styles

Joseph II's war against old customs paralleled larger conflicts of ideas in his realm and elsewhere. The baroque world order that underlay seventeenth and eighteenth century civilization was falling apart. Such a breakdown extended deep into the human psyche, with liberating—and often frightening—impact on religion and all of the arts.

Not only was reason praised by the Enlightenment, but also a new and somewhat contradictory cult of the emotions. Music became more impulsive and democratic, and national trends began to replace Italian-dominated formulas so dear to the

Farewell to the Old Order

W. H. Hadow in Volume IV of The Oxford History of Music *contrasts the old and the new of the changing social and political times:*

"Here then we have a background for the musical history of the period: a society brilliant, light, artificial, sumptuous and ceremonial, lavish in expenditure . . . a Church which appeared to have outlived its creed and forgotten its duties; its lower offices ranking with the peasant and the lackey, the higher given up to principalities and powers: a *bourgeoisie* solid, coarse, ill-educated but sound at heart, beginning, as the century waned, to feel its strength and purpose for its coming democracy. It is impossible to over-estimate the importance to music of the social and political changes which culminated in the decade of Revolution. They meant that the old regime had been tried and found wanting, that the standard of taste was no longer an aristocratic privilege, that the doors of the salon should be thrown open, and that art should emerge into a larger and more liberal atmosphere."

The advertisement for the Vienna premiere of The Abduction from the Seraglio *dated July 16, 1782.*

aristocracy. Historian Kurt Frank Reinhardt places Haydn and Mozart among these innovators "of a popular musical style, breaking down the artificial barriers that separated the different classes of the German population and finding a way not only to the heart and soul of the people at large, but demonstrating at the same time the possibility of a homogeneous [uniform] and indigenous [native] German culture."[19]

Other Social Changes

Another historian points to the movement known as *Sturm und Drang* (Storm and Stress) as a harbinger of change. The works of poets and friends Johann Wolfgang von Goethe, well-known for his *Faust,* and Friedrich von Schiller were symptomatic, especially Schiller's. He had fled to the German cultural center at Weimar after serving as military physician under the tyrannical duke of Württemberg. Said his hero in the 1781 drama *The Robbers,* a psychological study of the rebellious personality, "Put me in front of an army of fellows like myself and Germany will be turned into a republic."[20]

Goethe was devoted to free thought, science, and civic progress. His fictitious hero Faust abandoned religion and pawned his immortal soul to the devil for the sake of knowledge, power, and pleasure. Not quite so emphatically as Goethe, other creative people also responded to the new age, whether in music or poetry or theater or statesmanship. At least in his bolder works—for example, the powerful opera *Don Giovanni*—Mozart joined them. It was a good, but because of the possibility for revolution, a dangerous, time to be alive.

A Fresh Start

Mozart's mature career fell within these years of change. By now anyone could sympathize with the woes of an ambitious virtuoso in his midtwenties returning to the drudgery of the archbishop's establishment. Even composing sacred music was hampered by the mandatory time limits Colloredo had imposed on masses and the so-called church sonata interludes that a genius might presumably dash off before breakfast.

Archbishop Colloredo resented freelancing by his employees as well. He treated members of his orchestra like cooks and butlers, as was common practice until Haydn and Beethoven upgraded the profession. While father Leopold Mozart managed to compromise, the son rebelled. Moreover, as he often griped, Salzburg's artistic resources lagged far behind what he had seen and heard elsewhere.

His great opportunity was the order for a full-length opera seria, *Idomeneo*, for Munich's winter carnival of 1781. The commission came from none other than the music-loving duke, Karl Theodore, formerly of Mannheim and now in power in the Bavarian capital. Moreover, many of the fine Mannheim instrumentalists whom Mozart knew had accompanied their duke to Munich. Thus Mozart would be among friends of known ability. Somehow he coaxed a leave from his archbishop to relocate temporarily to work on the *Idomeneo* score and with the performers. Predictably, his long sojourn caused further squabbles back home.

In spite of favorable beginnings, the completed opera abounded with problems. The women of the cast were excellent, but one of the male leads—Anton Raaff, an old acquaintance—was an artist past his prime. On the other hand, the young countertenor lacked experience. The libretto furnished by Varesco, a fellow Salzburger, lacked dramatic flair until Mozart improved it.

When finally produced after several delays, this opera seemed—and still seems—an uneven but marvelous work. To modern ears the long recitatives by one-dimensional stick figures would make hard listening. But many of the solos are gorgeous, and instrumental color, especially for wind instruments, is sumptuous throughout. Notable are the storm music, the threat of a sea monster, Neptune's words from underground, and ensembles for multiple voices far ahead of anything Italian opera had

Karl Theodore was Duke of Mannheim, Elector of the Holy Roman Empire, and patron of the best orchestra in Europe in the 1770s. He later moved to Munich and became ruler of Bavaria.

A Twentieth Century View of *Idomeneo*

In Mozart: His Character/His Work, *the prominent musicologist Alfred Einstein accounts for the unusual power of* Idomeneo:

"Mozart is not afraid of anything, even of the shipwreck scene, with its two contrasting choruses, one on the stage and one in the distance. The Quartet, No. 21, in which Idamante takes his leave . . . is the first really great ensemble in the history of the *opera seria*. Mozart no longer wrote any everyday numbers. To us it seems as if in *Idomeneo* he had brought a series of his best vocal concert numbers [recitatives, arias, and ensembles] into a dramatic connection and united them by means of an imposing and uncanny overture, choral scenes, and instrumental pieces. Yet for its period *Idomeneo* was, in operatic form, a drama of unprecedented freedom and daring."

The first measures of a solo from Idomeneo *in Mozart's handwriting show accompanying instruments and vocal line. The full score would contain hundreds of such pages.*

known previously. Particularly impressive are several choruses demonstrating the young composer's indebtedness to Gluck's operas *Alceste* and *Orpheus and Eurydice*.

In short, Mozart had worked wonders with ancient materials. The plot depicts King Idomeneo returning from the Trojan War to save his storm-battered ship by vowing to sacrifice the first person who greets him on his home island of Crete. The unaware victim happens to be his only son, Idamante.

Though horrified, the two resolve to fulfill this vow. Just in time, however, the sea god intervenes. Human sacrifice is forbidden, and as punishment for such a rash pledge, the father must abdicate. His son and his son's bride, the lovely Trojan captive Ilia, will now inherit the throne. Mercy prevails and the kingdom is secured.

If these people's names sound like diseases, that's one of the problems in grand opera. After judicious cuts and the recasting of Idamante as a tenor, *Idomeneo* can still delight a serious audience. Long neglected,

The title page of an Idomeneo *libretto for the opera's Munich premiere in 1781 credits Theodore as patron, Varesco for the lyrics, and Mozart for the music.*

In this mid-nineteenth century illustration, harem boss Osmin objects to the Pasha pardoning his foes at the climax of The Abduction of the Seraglio.

A city square in Vienna about 1760 as portrayed by the eminent Venetian painter Canaletto.

it has appeared in modern opera houses, perhaps as the best of a dying breed—a sort of musical brontosaurus.

Its creator never lost faith in his old-fashioned effort. The dramatic device of the Oedipal conflict between father and son is eternally workable, as it was in Mozart's own life. The issue of human sacrifice, doubly painful when one's own child is threatened, has alarmed audiences ever since people have known the stories of Abraham and his son Isaac or Jephtha and his daughter in the Old Testament. In fact, Mozart loved and respected *Idomeneo* sufficiently to produce a shortened version in Vienna several years later. Though successful in Munich, the full opera did not travel easily, as few other orchestras could cope with its difficult score.

From Munich he was ordered to rush to Vienna to make a state visit with the rest of Colloredo's staff. Inevitable disputes arose when Colloredo wanted Mozart seated with menial servants. Also, this employer denied him a chance to earn extra money through recitals at the homes of wealthy patrons. An irate letter from Mozart to his father Leopold of June 13, 1781, recounts that famous culminating insult at the hand of—or rather the foot of—Count Arco, the archbishop's chamberlain:

> Instead of taking my petition [for release from Colloredo's service] or procuring me an audience... Count Arco hurls me out of the room and gives me a kick on my behind. Well, that means in our language that Salzburg is no longer the place for me, except to give me a favorable opportunity of returning the Count's kick, even if it should have to be in the public street. I

A CHANGED LIFE IN CHANGING TIMES ■ 47

> **The Perils of Performance**
>
> *This excerpt from Mozart's letter to Leopold of July 20, 1782, is quoted in Emily Anderson's book. It describes the tumultuous second performance of* Abduction.
>
> "Can you really believe it, but yesterday there was an even stronger cabal [plot] against it than on the first evening! The whole first act was accompanied by hissing. But indeed they could not prevent the loud shouts of 'bravo' during the arias. I was relying on the closing trio, but as ill-luck would have it, Fischer went wrong, which made Dauer go wrong too; and Adamberger alone could not sustain the trio [these were the male stars], with the result that the whole effect was lost.... I was in such a rage ... that I was simply beside myself and said at once that I would not let the opera be given again without having a short rehearsal for the singers."

am not demanding any satisfaction from the Archbishop, for he cannot procure it for me in the way in which I intend to obtain it for myself. But one of these days I shall write to the Count and tell him what he may confidently expect from me as soon as my good fortune allows me to meet him.[21]

Of course the tiff with Colloredo's underling disturbed Leopold, who repeatedly warned his son of the perils of striking out on his own. But there was no turning back now, and good luck favored the jobless Wolfgang with an opera commission worth nearly ten thousand dollars in modern buying power. As a new sovereign asserting himself, Joseph II intended this musical venture and others to encourage native productions (sung in German, whatever the plot setting) as alternatives to the foreign Italian opera then fashionable.

Mozart's contribution to this pro-German movement, *The Abduction from the Seraglio*, used a text by the mediocre poet Stephanie, who had helped procure the commission. It dramatized the attempt of a young European aristocrat, Belmont, to free his lady love Constanza from the clutches of a Turkish pasha, or official, holding her captive. The fat harem boss Osmin, who wears a turban as large as a beach ball, supplies comic relief in spite of himself. Though Osmin is made drunk, against his religion, by Belmont's helper Pedrillo in an attempt to rescue Constanza, the plot is foiled and its perpetrators fear for their lives. Unexpectedly, the pasha (a speaking, not singing, role) teaches these Christians a lesson in mercy by freeing Belmont, Pedrillo, and Constanza, and providing a boat for their homeward journey, even though Belmont happens to be the son of an old enemy.

The musical score is alternately humorous and lavish in Mozart's best manner; triangles and drums add an ethnic Middle Eastern touch. He admitted to embroidering the character Constanza's role with needless coloratura at the urging of the prima donna (female lead). Though a musical purist at heart, he conscientiously honed musical pieces to the skill and range of particular soloists and made other adjustments for the sake of theatrical effects.

An initially hostile audience could not prevent *Abduction* from a long run of forty-one performances in Vienna alone and numerous others elsewhere during the composer's lifetime. Just the first two days saw a gross income of twelve hundred florins. This sum, however, went to the theater, because Mozart had already received his modest wages. Continued success after a troubled second-night performance and contacts with influential noblemen and a few concerts assured him that he could make a living in his adopted city. In spite of his lack of seniority among the more prominent musicians in Vienna, and of opposition by a good-old-boy network (part real, part imagined), Vienna resembled the Promised Land to Mozart.

Wedding Bells at Last

Both before and after the production of his opera, the homeless newcomer had lodgings with the same Webers he had known in Mannheim. The Weber girls, whose father had died, were also seeking better opportunities in the larger city. Leopold had always considered them little better than gypsies, and now the reports of

St. Stephen's Cathedral in Vienna, site of Constanza's and Wolfgang's marriage in 1782 and Mozart's funeral nine years later.

growing intimacy between his son and the younger sister, Constanza, alarmed him. She was a vocalist and pianist of moderate ability but, according to Wolfgang, the family's best housekeeper.

Obviously marriage with Constanza was on Mozart's mind. One of his letters declared that "the voice of nature speaks as loud in me as in others, louder, perhaps, than in many a big strong lout of a fellow."[22] Constanza's mother was as eager for the union to happen as was Mozart's father to block it, and she forced Wolfgang to sign a contract that carried financial penalties if he broke the informal engagement.

To her credit, Constanza tore up this paper when Frau Weber left the room. Even without Leopold's blessing (which arrived a day late, and grudgingly, along with greetings from Nannerl), vows were

A Future Wife

In a letter dated December 15, 1781, Wolfgang described Constanza to his father (from Emily Anderson, The Letters of Mozart and His Family*).*

"My good, dear Constanza is the martyr of the family and, probably for that very reason, is the kindest-hearted, the cleverest and, in short, the best of them all. She makes herself responsible for the whole household and yet in their opinion she does nothing right.... But before I cease to plague you with my chatter, I must make you better acquainted with the character of my dear Constanza. She is not ugly, but at the same time far from beautiful. Her whole beauty consists in two little black eyes and a pretty figure. She has no wit, but she has enough common sense to enable her to fulfill her duties as a wife and mother. It is a downright lie that she is inclined to be extravagant. On the contrary, she is accustomed to be shabbily dressed.... Moreover she understands housekeeping and has the kindest heart in the world. I love her and she loves me with all her heart."

Constanza (née Weber) Mozart, Wolfgang's wife from 1782 until his death. Constanza later married Georg Nissen, a Danish diplomat who co-authored, along with Constanza, the first complete biography of Mozart.

Mozart's two surviving children, (left) Franz Xaver and Karl Thomas. Franz became a composer of moderate ability while Karl became a wealthy, highly respected government bureaucrat.

spoken in the great church of St. Stephen's on August 4, 1782.

Nine years after his wedding, the funeral service for the composer would be held in this same church, terminating a marriage that has been debated for its compatibility, its benefit to either party, and the amount of real love involved. The first child was born the following June but lived only a few months. Of Constanza and Wolfgang's six offspring, only Karl Thomas (born in 1784) and Franz Xaver (born in 1791, half a year before Wolfgang's death) grew to adulthood. A high rate of infant mortality was expected in those days due to the many untreatable childhood diseases.

Anyway, and for good or ill, Mozart had at last established his domestic and professional life in the city of his choice. An unpredictable nine years lay ahead—both for him and for his country.

Chapter 4

Boom Times

From 1782 through 1786, Mozart's obligation was to survive and to provide for his wife and children. But he was determined not to have to do so in the slavish manner of Salzburg. We will see how far this determination took him in Vienna, the great city on the Danube.

His association with sophisticated members of Joseph II's circle helped. Most useful of these contacts was Baron von Swieten, a Handel and Bach enthusiast who held Sunday morning gatherings at his town house to run through baroque scores. Even earlier, while *The Abduction from the Seraglio* was being prepared, Mozart appeared before Joseph to compete with the famous keyboard virtuoso Muzio Clementi, an Italian in the midst of a renowned international career. Mozart won the contest, and though praised by Clementi, did not return the compliment in a letter he wrote to Leopold soon after the event:

> Now a word about Clementi. He is an excellent cembalo [harpsichord] player, but that is all. He has great facility with his right hand. His star passages are thirds. Apart from this, he has not a farthing's worth of taste or feeling; he is a mere *mechanicus* [technician]. . . .

A nineteenth-century artist imagines Mozart composing in his room in Vienna's Kahlenburg.

> ### Reaching the Public on Two Levels
>
> *Emily Anderson quotes from Wolfgang's letter to his father of December 28, 1782, describing his style in several new piano concertos:*
>
> "[The concertos] are a happy medium between what is too easy and too difficult; they are very brilliant, pleasing to the ear, and natural, without being vapid [uninteresting]. There are passages here and there from which the connoisseurs [experts] alone can derive satisfaction; but these passages are written in such a way that the less learned cannot fail to be pleased, though without knowing why.... I am now finishing too the piano arrangement of [*Abduction from the Seraglio*], which is about to be published."

[The emperor] was extremely pleased with me. He was very gracious, said a great deal to me privately, and even mentioned my [upcoming] marriage.[23]

Though sociable and fond of talk, dancing, and parties, Mozart's frank criticism of fellow musicians earned him enemies. In contrast, when he found greatness, as in some of the music of Haydn, who was soon to become a friend and mentor, his praise was generous. The following incident is typical:

> A new quartet of Haydn's was being performed before a large company. Kozeluch [another composer], who was standing beside Mozart, began finding fault first with one thing, then with another, and at last he exclaimed with the impudent effrontery of his kind: "I should never have done it that way!" "Nor should I," replied Mozart, "and do you know why? Because neither you nor I would ever have had such a good idea."[24]

Mozart's first great public successes after his *Seraglio* were a series of piano concertos with himself as soloist, using freelance musicians and selling tickets at the door or subscriptions in advance. Occasionally he wrote somewhat easier concertos for pupils, with lighter scoring adjusted to lesser skills, or optional scores that could be performed with string orchestras or even as chamber music. In these works he proudly steered a middle course between technical finesse, or skill, and popular appeal.

Until the novelty wore off a few years later, the magic of piano-and-orchestra ensembles dazzled ordinary audiences while impressing experts. They became his bread-and-butter products for a time. Many of these works were neglected in the nineteenth century; now the concertos are performed and analyzed almost to death. In other composers' hands, such works can become tinkly parlor entertainment or athletic display; but as perfected by Mozart, surface glitter combines with profound feeling. The moods range from military pomp to glimpses of beauty beyond earthly limits. Examination of the underlying technique discloses every trick of the trade: saucy conversation between soloist and group, hidden counterpoint, shifts of accent and key, and occasional writing that permits the soloist to improvise or embellish as she or he wishes.

Mozart practically invented the true concerto, and his mastery of the form has seldom been outshone by later talents to the present day. After hearing Mozart's K. 466 in D minor, for which he wrote cadenzas, the great Beethoven declared that "none of us alive can do so well." If Beethoven and Brahms wrote greater symphonies, Mozart's piano concertos, together with his operas, remain the standard for judging the work of anyone else.

Yet these masterworks were crowded into a relatively few peak years. While creating them, Mozart was also a conscientious piano teacher. Most of his clientele were fashionable young ladies. In a few cases he also accepted composition students. Surviving exercises show his teaching methods: tunes to be harmonized, tunes to be built upon a given line in the bass, harmonic analyses of existing scores. Of course he welcomed the supplementary income from teaching, as well as receiving the incidental gold watches or purses of money from recitals in private salons, where he was for the time in great demand. Like present-day teachers, he soon discovered that students skip lessons. Therefore he required that his fees be paid by the month, in advance, with no refunds for absenteeism.

Family Life

The relative prosperity that Mozart achieved in these years allowed his marriage to settle down into comfortable intimacy marked by regular childbirths, though only one child born during this period, Karl Thomas, born in 1784, lived into adulthood. When income declined, the small family would take smaller lodgings; when luck turned, they would rent a fancy apartment with good furniture and more servants.

Skeptical Papa Leopold was lured from Salzburg for a long visit in the spring of 1785 to see his new grandchild and observe the Mozarts at work and play. Evidently Nannerl's marriage and removal to another town had left him lonesome back home.

In 1785, Leopold visited Constanza, Wolfgang, and his new grandson, Karl Thomas.

He must have found a better-run Vienna household than expected, though in a letter to Nannerl he did comment on its incessant activity:

> "We never get to bed before one o'clock and I never get up before nine. We lunch at two or half past. The weather is horrible. Every day there are concerts; and the whole time is given up to teaching, music, composing and so forth. I feel rather out of it all. If only the concerts were over! It is impossible for me to describe the rush and bustle. Since my arrival your brother's fortepiano has been taken at least a dozen times to the theatre or to some other house. He has had a large fortepiano pedal made, which stands under the instrument and is about two feet longer and extremely heavy.[25]

The keyboard instrument Leopold mentions comprised five octaves and sounded crisper than modern pianos. Unfortunately, its pedal board has disappeared. Whether this attachment merely had the effect of doubling the bass sound or operated independently like an organ's pedals is arguable.

Other tidbits from this same letter included praise for the cooking at the once-despised Frau Weber's home. Was a reconciliation possible? Also, Leopold estimated that Wolfgang could now put two thousand guldens (forty thousand dollars) in the bank "if my son has no debts to pay." The gulden was worth about twenty dollars in today's money.

It was during this visit that Leopold joined the Freemasons, to which his son already belonged. Mozart convinced the father to join, and also persuaded Franz Joseph Haydn to follow suit. Perhaps, Wolf-

Mozart acquired this forte-piano in 1784 and used it for composing, for teaching at home and for concerts away from home. It is now displayed at the Mozarteum in Salzburg.

gang hoped to increase the connection between Haydn and himself.

The young composer's regard for the older Haydn speaks through Mozart's music written at that time, both in structure and the way musical themes are developed. To acknowledge this influence, Mozart finished six quartets, using months of hard work in contrast to his usual speed. Their respectful dedication to Haydn surely gratified an esteemed master who was just now emerging from obscurity at the Esterhazy estate to spend more time in town and shortly to travel abroad.

An informal musical combo that included Wolfgang, Haydn himself, and other musical cronies had already sampled these

A Debt of Gratitude

Otto Eric Deutsch's collection of Mozart documents reproduces this dedication of the six quartets to Haydn as it appeared on the title page of the September 1, 1785, edition of the music. The children referred to here are Mozart's quartets:

"To my dear friend Haydn,

A father who had resolved to send his children out into the great world took it to be his duty to confide them to the protection and guidance of a very celebrated Man, especially when the latter by good fortune was at the same time his best Friend. Here they are then, O great Man and my dearest Friend, these six children of mine. They are, it is true, the fruit of long and laborious endeavour, yet the hope inspired in me by several Friends that it may be at least partly compensated encourages me, and I flatter myself that this offspring will serve to afford me some solace one day. You yourself, dearest friend, told me of your satisfaction with them during your last Visit to this Capital. It is this indulgence above all which urges me to commend them to you and encourages me to hope that they will not seem to you altogether unworthy of your favour. May it therefore please you to receive them kindly and to be their Father, Guide and Friend! From this moment I resign to you all my rights in them, begging you however to look indulgently upon the defects which the partiality of a Father's eye may have concealed from me, and in spite of them to continue in your generous Friendship for him who so greatly values it, in expectation of which I am, with all my Heart, my dearest Friend, your most Sincere Friend, W. A. Mozart. Vienna, 1 September 1785."

Mozart dedicated his six quartets to his friend and supporter Franz Josef Haydn (left).

An artist's conception of Mozart and his older friend Haydn sharing professional ideas.

works at home. A proud Leopold wrote Nannerl that "Haydn said to me 'Before God and as an honest man I tell you that your son is the greatest composer known to me either in person or by name. He has taste and, what is more, the most profound knowledge of composition.'"[26]

With such recommendations, how could a new star in the Viennese heavens fade? These half-dozen quartets outshone anything by Haydn or anything else by Mozart himself to date. Despite difficulties for performers, the music sold well, earning Mozart 100 ducats. Keys and emotions vary; violins, viola, and cello sing eloquently; and modern discords crop up in the opening of the last written of the set, the C Major, or "Dissonant," quartet.

Together they became the graduate school for Beethoven's experiments in the same form a few years later. When Mozart, Haydn, and fellow composers Dittersdorf and Vanhal gathered to rehearse such stuff, think what a tape recording of their jam sessions would cost in the twentieth century!

Although untrustworthy as a supposed depiction of Haydn and Mozart playing a duet for violin and keyboard, this illustration reflects home music making in the 1780s.

BOOM TIMES ■ 57

Barbers, Maidservants, Counts, and Countesses

Besides producing chamber music and concertos, Mozart labored through the fall and winter of 1785–1786 on his great comic opera, *The Marriage of Figaro*. *Figaro*'s origins are complicated. Mozart had always loved vocal music (music for the voice), and experience with early grand opera and church music readied him for a big commission after the 1782 success of *The Abduction from the Seraglio*. But the German-language *Singspiel* to which that work belonged had not become popular, and Joseph II, reluctantly realizing this, had allowed Italian productions to be performed more. As a stickler for good librettos, Mozart had tried and junked a couple of new examples. Nothing appealed until Lorenzo Da Ponte came forward.

Da Ponte was an adventurer who was born Jewish, converted to Christianity,

Poet and world-traveller Lorenzo Da Ponte (1749–1838) was the librettist for The Marriage of Figaro, Don Giovanni, *and* Cosi fan Tutte.

Figaro Is Angry

Even in translation, Figaro's rebelliousness in Beaumarchais's original play comes through. His Marriage of Figaro *was forbidden performance until 1785, seven years after it was written:*

"As a noble lord, you [Count Almaviva] view yourself as a superior creature. Your rank, money, and official appointments make you swell with pride. But do you deserve such privileges? All you needed to do was get born; except for *that,* you're no better than anyone else! Meanwhile, by God, I was lost in the mob. I battled for mere survival with more intelligence and cleverness than it takes to govern all of Spain!"

temporarily became a monk (and a bad one), then a self-taught poet who supplied texts for opera composers in Vienna, often juggling several projects simultaneously. He and Mozart selected a script based on the second of French playwright Beaumarchais's two works about Figaro. The first, *The Barber of Seville,* had already been set to music by crowd-pleaser Giovanni Paisiello, an Italian in Vienna with whom Mozart remained on good terms. Ignoring threats of official censorship because of their scenario's revolutionary theme, the collaborators forged ahead. If Da Ponte's account can be trusted, he personally got the emperor's permission to stage his and Mozart's version of *Figaro,* with the condition that Da Ponte alter the plot to eliminate some radical ideas regarding the aristocracy.

Regardless of this "laundering," revolutionary undertones survived. Even though its artificial plot borrows from the old stage-comedy devices of mistaken identities and predictable farce, the characters are not at all stereotyped, and the emotions are plausible. As one example, the curtain rises on valet-handyman Figaro doing nothing heroic or especially comic. Instead this sensible husband-to-be sings "cinque, deici, trenta" (surely the least poetic opera opener ever) while measuring the room he and the maid Susanna will occupy after their wedding. Meanwhile, she tries on the hat for her bridal outfit.

Their domestic scene begins a series of hilarious confrontations that progressively involve and demoralize Count Almaviva (Susanna and Figaro's employer) and his entire retinue, from the countess to the drunken gardener. Our lecherous count wants Susanna for himself, although he is married to a gorgeous lady who weeps about her unrequited love for her husband.

The advertisement for the Vienna opening of The Marriage of Figaro *on May 1, 1786.*

Two scenes from The Marriage of Figaro, *probably based on a Prague production in the 1790s.*

An aging scold named Marcellina, housekeeper of this disorderly estate, presses Figaro to marry *her* instead, or else repay money he had foolishly borrowed.

The climactic third act finds Susanna offering Marcellina a bag of gold (her own dowry) to cancel the debt of Figaro, her betrothed. Figaro, however, has meanwhile discovered through a forgotten birthmark that Marcellina is his *mother* rather than a potential spouse, and that huffing-and-puffing Dr. Bartolo, the woman's lover long ago, is thus his *father.* Upon the discovery, newly united mother and son hug.

Enraged by the sight of her fiancé hugging another female, Susanna slaps Figaro, before being told the real situation. Twice she listens to others of the ensemble recite, one by one in rising pitches, "sua madre?" or "sua padre?" ("your mother?" "your father?") to which she echoes the same words in bewilderment until the truth dawns. All of this occurs as six people warble at once, each voice expressing feelings that suit its owner, until harmony is restored.

Years afterward, widowed Constanza recalled this sextet as Mozart's favorite number in the entire opera, as it still is for many fans. And if we think it sounds elaborate, the last act drifts even closer to utter confusion. Among other mix-ups at a garden party after the wedding, Susanna and the countess exchange costumes in order to test the fidelity of their mates. Figaro sees through the trick, but Almaviva proceeds to woo his own wife, taking her for the maid he has been hustling all day. When this deception is revealed, the count begs forgiveness, and love wins out as the curtain descends after some of the most beautiful melodies ever written:

Mozart's Competition

W. J. Turner's Mozart: The Man and His Works *summarizes the public's reception of* The Marriage of Figaro (Le Nozze di Figaro):

"On May 1, 1786, *Le Nozze di Figaro* was first performed at the National Theater in Vienna. It was a success, but no extraordinary success; certainly nothing to compare with the success, a few months later, of Martin's *Cosa Rara,* which quite overshadowed *Figaro* both in popular estimation and in that of 'connoisseurs' such as the Emperor Joseph II and the composer Dittersdorf. For example, during the whole of the two following years of 1787 and 1788 *Figaro* was not once performed in Vienna. It was first performed in Berlin in 1790; but although praised by the critics, the public preferred the operas of Martin and Dittersdorf. It was a complete failure in Italy, where it was first produced, only after Mozart's death, in 1792. . . . On the other hand, it was performed in Prague in the winter of 1786–87 with tremendous success. . . ."

Fancy dress, a nobleman up to his usual tricks: what is radical about *that*? But even after Da Ponte sanitized the script, Figaro's statements annoyed conservatives. The valet asserts the equality of ordinary citizens and nobles, just as Mozart had in real life—if not in social rank, then certainly in basic human rights. Figaro never acts servile, except as a joke. Of course he loathes the count's *droit de seigneur*, the medieval right of a lord to the first night with a vassal's new bride—a nasty but supposedly abolished custom.

This mere lackey outsmarts his rival and is in turn outsmarted by Susanna, who constantly schemes her way into and out of trouble. She is witty, even aggressive at times, but chaste and dignified when need be, and her mistress regards her almost as family.

And this elegant, sorrowing countess is also a new breed. Of bourgeois rather than noble origin, she prefers so-called family values to the old sex games of the privileged classes. At least this holds true of Mozart's and his partner's version, though Beaumarchais's countess had behaved less well.

Evidently *Figaro* was more suitable for the future than for its own day. Its Vienna debut was moderately upbeat but soon eclipsed by lesser operas. Perhaps a great artist is never fully appreciated on home turf.

Mozart Magic

During this same period Mozart wrote one of his greatest but least popular piano concertos, K. 503 in C major. Like several other grand concertos, it adds trumpets and tympani (kettle drums) to the basic flutes, oboes or clarinets, bassoons, French horns, and stringed instruments. A fanfare opens the longest symphonic movement anywhere in this composer's output. Here, as elsewhere, sonata form hangs great variety onto a logical framework, as though a mighty skeleton holds up a beautiful and agile body. Or to use another image, it strikes the balance between "head" and "heart" that artists seek but don't always achieve.

In spite of K. 503's grandeur, most listeners prefer *Figaro*'s showcase of vivid emotions. Almost everyone recognizes the valet's marchlike ditty in act 1 as he strides across the stage, imaginary musket at his shoulder, to taunt the page boy, Cherubino, who has been drafted into the army by Count Almaviva as punishment for innocent and not-so-innocent pranks:

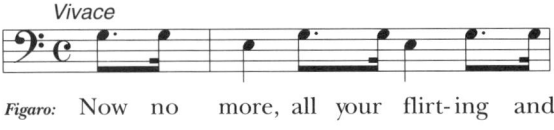

Very different is a lament the neglected countess sings to a tune Mozart had used earlier in a religious context:

The original mellow Italian begins "Porgi, amor, qualche ristoro al mio duolo, a' miei sospir. . . ." English translations for modern productions sound less poetic, though they are needed for full comprehension. Notice, too, the flowing, weaving rhythm. Harmony is fairly straightforward. When it is analyzed, we find the simple strong melody of hymns or folk tunes; yet the melody affects us strangely—for reasons understood only by the man who wrote it.

This mention of contemporary music makes us wonder how Mozart might respond to the twentieth century if he were to have a second life. Of course his harmonies would grow wilder and less predictable. Having experimented with glass harmonicas and mechanical organs, he might try electronics, while avoiding mere technical stunts because "music must always be *music*." Both Lincoln Center and Broadway could exploit his artistry, particularly in operetta and comic opera. We like to imagine him earning millions from radio and TV—but at the same time, such fashionable prosperity seems out of character.

In the 1780s, though, he was a greater genius than most of his audiences guessed. Because he sought fame and recognition, he had set up shop in one of the great centers of Germanic culture. And yet, looking back, one wishes he and Constanza had accepted invitations to London, a city he remembered from childhood. There he would have faced less rivalry from envious second-rate musicians and, perhaps, lived longer.

For several reasons, including Leopold's opposition, this never happened, though Haydn utilized a similar chance to gain freedom from haughty aristocrats and fickle commoners, and in England wrote symphonies rivaling Mozart's best. Before departing, this generous "elder statesman of music" once more lauded his protégé to the skies. A letter of December 1787 to an official in Prague urged the city to find a position worthy of Mozart. As usual, the powers-that-be paid little attention, even though the two operas staged there were hits for a while:

> If I were able to impress the soul of every music-lover, and more especially the great ones, with my own understanding of and feeling for Mozart's incomparable works, so *profound* and so full of *musical intelligence*... then the nations would vie with each other to possess such a jewel within their encircling walls. Let Prague hold fast to the precious man—but also reward him.... It makes me angry to think that this *unique* Mozart has not yet found an appointment at some imperial or royal court! Forgive me if I stray from my path. I love the man too much.[27]

Chapter 5
Good Luck and Bad

After the disappointing reaction *Figaro* received in Vienna, an Italian troupe presented *Figaro* in Prague, the provincial capital of Bohemia, to such acclaim late in 1786 that Wolfgang and Constanza were invited to the city for a month's stay. Prague was a smaller, less pretentious version of Vienna. Its music-loving citizens lacked the know-it-all snobbery of upper-class Austrians. Mozart conducted several *Figaro*s on his own, as well as a new symphony, now known as the *Prague*, composed for the occasion and his finest so far.

The couple made many friends in that city. Mozart wrote to an acquaintance back home about observing a public dance "with the greatest pleasure while these people flew about in sheer delight to the music . . . arranged for quadrilles and waltzes. . . . Nothing is played, sung or whistled but 'Figaro.' Nothing, nothing but 'Figaro.' Certainly a great honor for me."[28]

His Prague impresario (producer), a certain Pasquale Bondini, liked the opera so much that he commissioned a new one on the spot. Surely the current share

A contemporary view of Prague, Mozart's favorite city. Prague hosted the second production of Figaro *and the premiere of* Don Giovanni.

Young Beethoven auditions before Mozart in this highly imaginative portrayal of the meeting between the two musicians.

from the profits of one thousand gulden (twenty thousand dollars) would ease the financial hardships that began to run the Mozarts into debt, and the new opera would earn one hundred ducats when completed. Their money crunch, while not yet chronic, was caused by the uneven income from a chancy occupation: solvent one month from ticket sales or fees from the sale of published scores, eating toast without jam the next.

After Mozart and Constanza returned to Austria, a shaggy-haired young man from Bonn in the Rhineland paid a call. This prodigy of the next generation, Ludwig van Beethoven by name, performed for Wolfgang and apparently earned high praise, though their meeting is not well documented. Whether or not Mozart formally instructed Beethoven after the visit is unknown, but Beethoven was abruptly called home for a family emergency and did not see Vienna again until the mid-1790s.

Beethoven later showed his regard for his predecessor by writing cadenzas for a Mozart concerto. Occasionally he also composed variations on Mozart tunes, including a good-humored echo of Don Giovanni's valet Leporello in the last and greatest of them, the so-called Diabelli Variations.

Sadly, Mozart would not live to enjoy such compliments. And he would need all of a son's strength of character at the reports of father Leopold's decline and death in May 1787. This man had served as parent, instructor, moral guide (not always successfully), business manager for the childhood tours, and role model for work habits, keen judgments, and (at times) feisty stubbornness. Though they had often argued over Constanza's fitness as a wife and over other matters, nobody else among Wolfgang's correspondents received so much mail from him—more than 250 surviving letters—about either personal troubles or shoptalk.

The sad news prompted several letters to Nannerl. "You can easily imagine, as our loss is equally great," Wolfgang wrote at first, "how pained I was by . . . the sudden death of our dearest father." Being too busy for a trip to Salzburg, Mozart accepted Nannerl's decision to put up Leopold's goods for public auction. "Rest assured, my dear," he added, "that if you desire a kind brother to love and protect you, you will find one in me on every occasion."[29] Evidently he accepted only a thousand gulden out of the inheritance, leaving the rest to Nannerl and her elderly husband, Baron von Sonnenburg.

The Statue That Came to Dinner

With these family affairs settled, Mozart was now free to tackle the new Prague opera commission with Da Ponte. Their inspiration was an ancient legend that first surfaced in a drama by the Spanish Renaissance author Tirso de Molina entitled *The Rascal of Seville*. From Molina the story passed down through the French playwright Molière and others to the minor poet Bertati, from whom Da Ponte cribbed—and improved—entire scenes, while adding his own.

In Da Ponte's version of the story, the text for Mozart's opera *Don Giovanni*, Tirso's antihero Giovanni scorns morality and deceives victims of both sexes, enjoying a rollicking good time meanwhile. Though reluctantly, this swashbuckler duels and kills the old father of a woman he had tried to seduce. After other adventures he extends an ironic dinner invitation to the graveyard statue of that dead man, while his valet Leporello pales at the thought.

At his clavier, Mozart envisions Don Giovanni's attempted assault of Donna Anna as the opera opens. Like many imaginative depictions of the composer's life and works, this painting was done many years later.

At this point Mozart gives the statue's deep monotone a frightening "Si!" with a nod of its marble head. Back at his villa, fearless Giovanni prepares to entertain this expected guest, whose heavy, approaching footsteps terrify the valet as well as Donna Elvira, a discarded gentlewoman who is begging Giovanni to reform.

The statue enters to the accompaniment of a scary D-minor chord for full orchestra. It walks mechanically, glowing weirdly. "Pentite, pentite," (repent, repent) it chants in slow, deep tones. Still defiant, Giovanni feels the statue's ice-cold, stony handclasp. In the Catholic faith, spurning an offer of salvation at the point of death is an unforgivable sin.

And Giovanni commits it. The statue exits, its warnings to repent ignored. A choir of demons exult as the evildoer, Giovanni, drops through a trapdoor into hellfire with a final bloodcurdling "Aaaah!" that his servant hiding under a table echoes.

Although he had aided and seldom criticized his master's escapades, Leporello (the name suggests "little rabbit") now resolves to lead a better life. Other members of the cast join a chorus of thanksgiving for the triumph of right over wrong.

The music of this puzzling opera excites audiences from its first measures to the last. According to Constanza, Mozart dashed off its splendid overture just the night before the first performance, obliging his orchestra to play it sight unseen. Its preview of motifs to follow did not reflect Mozart's former habits. Leporello's first act aria, listing his master's conquests—including "a thousand and three" women in Spain alone—is a sure-fire applause getter for any bass able to convey its gleeful mockery.

In the duet "La ci darem la mano" (Put your little hand in mine), Giovanni courts the peasant lass Zerlina, hoping to add her to his list of romantic conquests. Donna Anna, daughter of the man slain in the duel, is given superb solos and important ensemble roles. She and her fiancé Don Ottavio, represent the final victory of more righteous but less interesting people over Giovanni's immoral life-style.

No matter how we despise his swinger's ethics, the man is appealing. A drinking song rendered at top speed shows his personality in all its tawdry glamor. It begins like this:

Theater set for the graveyard scene in Don Giovanni, *from an early production.*

GOOD LUCK AND BAD ■ 67

Hap-py with vi-no, reel-ing and woo-zy, for a big par-ty, this is the place

The climax of *Don Giovanni* remains one of the great moments in all drama. Ever since the memorable Prague premiere, directors have reinvented Giovanni's doom. After the statue's unsuccessful attempt to reform him, Giovanni can be swallowed by a stage trapdoor (the usual method), clutched by batlike creatures, plunged into make-believe flames at the rear of the stage, whisked off by flying devils on wires, or (thanks to film technology) burned to a crisp with laser beams. Take your pick.

Even without laser beams, Prague was overwhelmed. As the news spread, Joseph II commanded the state theater in Vienna to premiere the opera there, for which occasion Mozart added and deleted some songs to satisfy local singers. In spite of fifteen performances, it was not popular, though shrewd critics called it a masterpiece. Berlin audiences heard it a few years later, with mixed reviews; Goethe praised the Weimar production, and *Don Giovanni* slowly made its way around the world. All major opera companies (except in Italy, a land of great singers, not great orchestras) now keep it in their repertoires. American public television recently gave it a Harlem setting that fit the mood of a society under siege. Modern directors and audiences tend to divide into those who view it as an old-fashioned morality play and those who see Giovanni (in spite of his wickedness) as an authentic rebel who would rather die than submit to other people's rules.

As another yield from their mixed success, Joseph II finally recognized Austria's greatest talent, if only nominally, by giving the composer an official appointment, as described in Stanley Sadie's book *The New Grove Mozart*:

> Mozart arrived back in Vienna in mid-November [1787] and was soon offered the post of court composer, or *Kammermusicus* at a salary of 800 gulden (Gluck, who had just died, had been paid 2000). He was apparently required

"Clasp your hand in mine," the stone guest orders Don Giovanni, who must now pay dearly for his sins.

to do little more than write dance music for court balls. Though not . . . a Kapellmeister at all except in a very loose sense, he could at least sign himself in the imperial and royal service. Clearly he welcomed this appointment, both for the dependable income associated with it and for its advancement of his standing in Viennese musical life.[30]

Though inadequate for a high standard of living in the expensive capital, this stipend of roughly sixteen thousand dollars annually represented a floor on which other earnings could support modest luxuries—*if* the Mozarts watched their budget.

Mozart reportedly declared that salary for writing dance hall music "too much for what I do, not enough for what I *could* do,"—a sad but appropriate claim, when we ponder it. And meaning to sound helpful, the emperor, who sometimes escaped politics to play chamber music, suggested that Vienna citizenry (including himself) could not grasp a style so subtle and difficult. On another occasion he *may* have said "Too many notes, my dear Mozart." Mozart is said to have replied, "On the contrary, Your Majesty, just the right number."[31]

A lean pocketbook in the wake of the *Don Giovanni* productions prompted the first of many pleas for loans to merchant and fellow mason Michael Puchberg. For a man of Mozart's caliber to beg for a hundred florins, or fifty, or anything his friend could spare, seems painfully unjust.

Besides other expenses, Constanza now needed therapy for various ailments at the

A Box-Office Hit

In Mozart: The Man and His Works, *W. J. Turner translates an account in a Vienna newspaper of Prague's reception of* Don Giovanni.

"On Monday, October 29, Kapellmeister Mozart's long-expected opera *Don Giovanni* . . . was performed by the Italian opera company of Prague. Musicians and connoisseurs are agreed in declaring that such a performance has never before been witnessed in Prague. Herr Mozart himself conducted and his appearance in the orchestra was the signal for cheers, which were renewed at his exit. The opera is exceedingly difficult of execution and the excellence of the representation, in spite of the short time allowed for studying the work, was the subject of general remark. The whole powers of both actors and orchestra were put forward to do honour to Mozart. Considerable expense was incurred for additional chorus and scenery. The enormous audience was a sufficient guarantee of the public favour."

Will the Real Don Giovanni Stand Up?

The modern scholar Hugh Ottaway in his book Mozart *mentions opposing views of Giovanni's behavior that persist into our own times:*

"It is not in the least surprising that *Don Giovanni* was condemned for its 'exaggerated, debauching contrasts.' There are aspects that are closer than *Figaro* to mainstream *opera buffa*—Leporello, for instance, is the traditional comic servant in a way that Figaro certainly is not—but there are other aspects which the Romantics . . . were able to seize upon and misinterpret from their own point of view. These differences may well reflect a conscious dualism in Mozart's and Da Ponte's response to the legend: on the one hand, sympathy with Giovanni's 'heroic' defiance of convention, but on the other, condemnation of the aristocratic libertine who destroys his fellow men."

Leporello cringes in terror as Giovanni challenges the cemetery statue of the murdered commandant.

> **Evidence of Hard Times**
>
> *Emily Anderson quotes this letter of June 1788, one of several from Mozart to Puchberg seeking a loan. In this instance the merchant noted on the letter that he "sent 100 gulden."*
>
> "DEAREST BROTHER! Your true friendship and brotherly love embolden me to ask a great favour of you. I still owe you eight ducats. Apart from the fact that at the moment I am not in a position to pay you back this sum, my confidence in you is so boundless that I dare to implore you to help me out with a hundred gulden until next week, when my concerts in the Casino are to begin. By that time I shall certainly have received my subscription money and shall then be able quite easily to pay you back 136 gulden with my warmest thanks. . . .
>
> Once more I ask your forgiveness for my importunity and with greetings to your esteemed wife I remain in true friendship and fraternal love, your most devoted brother W. A. MOZART"

Baden health resort. Critics have accused her of extravagance and hypochondria, and that she sought vacations from a difficult spouse, and flirted with other men. Still, the records show that at one time her leg ulcers were possibly life-threatening. Moreover, this so-called silly woman was able to repay a very large accumulated debt after Wolfgang's death through shrewd management of his estate.

But we cannot unscramble the Mozarts' private life. Whether they were constantly devoted or occasionally unfaithful, their marriage endured to the very end. That Wolfgang sometimes worried about Constanza's behavior is revealed by letters like the one of April 16, 1789, containing several do's and don'ts:

> Dear little wife, I have a number of requests to make.
>
> (1) I beg you not to be melancholy.
>
> (2) *to take care of your health* and *to beware of* the spring breezes.
>
> (3) not to go out walking alone—and preferably not to *go out walking* at all.
>
> (4) to feel absolutely assured of my love. Up to the present I have not written a single letter to you without placing your dear portrait before me.
>
> (5) I beg you in your conduct not only to be careful of your honour and mine, but also to consider appearances. Do not be angry with me for asking this. You ought to love me even more for thus valuing our honour.[32]

Hoping to recoup finances, Mozart planned a series of subscription (selling tickets in advance) concerts, possibly featuring three new symphonies. Of these works, No. 39 in E-flat is mellow and serene, while powerful No. 40 in G minor sounds perplexed and nervous. The composer may have heard only No. 40 in a live performance, and it exists in two orchestrations—with and without clarinets. (Unfortunately, Mozart's subscription plan failed when only the reliable Baron von Swieten purchased tickets.)

The last of the set, No. 41 in C major (the *Jupiter*, but not so named by its creator) radiates an almost godly brilliance, starting with the first movement's theme, which is a perfect example of his question-and-answer pattern and, in this case, the alteration of masculine strength and feminine grace:

The *Jupiter*'s slow movement unreels sinuous melodies, very richly scored, in a country mood that possibly influenced Beethoven's *Pastorale* Symphony. The minuet-and-trio portion moves too quickly for dancing, and the finale's themes chase each other helter-skelter before they fuse into a coda's five-voice counterpoint. Such rabbit-out-of-a-hat tricks came easily to a

---

A Father Disapproves

Always the worried father, Leopold writes to Nannerl on March 1, 1787, about his son's plans to travel abroad. The quote is taken from Emily Anderson's Letters of Mozart and His Family:

"As for your brother I hear that he is back in Vienna. I had no reply to the letter I sent to him at Prague. The English company told me that he made a thousand gulden there, that Leopold, his last boy, has died, and that, as I had gathered, he wants to travel to England but that his pupil [Thomas Atwood, a young English composer] is first going to procure a definite engagement for him in London, I mean, a contract to compose an opera or a subscription concert, etc.... But no doubt after I sent him a fatherly letter, saying that he would gain nothing by a journey in summer, as he would arrive in England at the wrong time, that he ought to have at least two thousand gulden in his pocket before taking such an expedition, and finally that, unless he had procured in advance some definite engagement in London, he would have to be prepared, no matter how clever he was, to be hard up at first at any rate, he has probably lost courage."

man who also improvised fugues on the organ—impossible stunts for mere mortals.

While gazing back toward Bach's style, Mozart sometimes looked forward to modern dissonance. The theme played in unison by the instruments that open the concerto K. 491 touches every note of the chromatic scale. Even though it sounds dissonant, however, it really is not because the home key of C minor lurks below the surface.

Mozart's interest in chamber music peaked in 1787 with the string quintets K. 515 and 516, which rank in quality with those last symphonies. The more familiar of the pair, in G minor, gallops along as feverishly as the symphony of the same key signature. Cellists love the first measures of the C major, K. 515, another "question and answer," as their instrument climbs a two-octave stairway into the embrace of violins and violas:

Though these quintets found a publisher, their difficulties limited sales despite Vienna's widespread musical literacy. Almost all educated persons could play and sing; opera or concerts were performed almost daily, except when townfolk scattered for the summer; nonprofessionals tried string quartets, piano-violin sonatas, and the like; and many opera tunes were transcribed for woodwinds or solo piano. Many of the easier Mozart scores were sold over-the-counter (not always to the composer's profit) even as public taste began to prefer more middlebrow, or somewhat cultured, entertainment.

Walking a tightrope between *ideal* and *popular* norms would exhaust anybody. Often in the past Mozart had discussed these difficulties with Papa Leopold, who was now no longer able to help.

Chapter 6
The Last Years

An eight-month lapse in paid public appearances through 1788 allowed Mozart to produce some compositions, but not for immediate gain. For a while Mozart wrote little, traveled more than he should have (missing Constanza dreadfully), and dodged bankruptcy by means of new loans. Stagecoaches took him to Dresden, Berlin, and Leipzig in April and May of 1789. Often he composed on the road. By an odd turn of events, his traveling companion, Prince Lichnowsky (later a Beethoven fan), borrowed money from *him.*

In Berlin the king of Prussia, member of a musical royal family, commissioned six new quartets from Mozart. This monarch played cello respectably and wanted that instrument emphasized. Only three of the "Prussian" quartets were ever delivered. Valuable for Mozart's musical development was his inspection in Bach's own Leipzig church of manuscripts of the late master's unpublished cantatas, now known worldwide. "Now, there's somebody a man can learn from," he is reported to have said—and he did learn, also from the great baroque composer Handel, in time to work their techniques into his last choral number, the *Requiem.*

But that masterpiece lay in the future. From Dresden, a note to Constanza in Vienna contained sentiments like these:

How to Be Popular

Mozart describes the musical taste of the people in a letter dated December 28, 1782, which is quoted in Emily Anderson:

"The golden mean of truth in all things is no longer either known or appreciated. In order to win applause one must write stuff which is so inane that a coachman could sing it, or so unintelligible that it pleases precisely because no sensible man can understand it."

Dearest little wife, if only I had a letter from you! If I were to tell you all the things I do with your dear portrait, I think that you would often laugh. For instance, when I take it out of its case, I say "Good day, Stanzerl!—Good day, little rascal... little turned up nose, little bagatelle"... and when I put it away again, I let it slip very slowly, saying all the time, "Nu—Nu—Nu—Nu!" with the peculiar *emphasis* which this word so full of meaning demands, and then just at the last, quickly, "Good night, little mouse, sleep well." Well, I suppose I have been writing something very foolish (to the world at all events); but to us who love each other so dearly, it is not foolish at all. Today is the sixth day since I left you, and by Heaven! it seems a year.[33]

His round-robin of German cities earned little money; neither did a trip to Frankfurt in the fall of 1789 for the crowning of the new emperor Leopold II after Joseph's death. The court favorite, Antonio Salieri, headed a large Viennese delegation to the coronation. This old rival, who had once tried to block the staging of *Figaro,* now had the good grace to include Mozart compositions in the festivities.

But Mozart himself was not formally invited. Thus, to make an appearance, he had to pay his own way, with the hope of recovering costs from ticket sales for personal appearances. With so many other shows in town, his were poorly attended. The piece he'd finished at top speed nevertheless bears the title *Coronation Concerto.* Its piano part was thinly notated because he could play from memory or else improvise where blanks occurred. Perhaps its

Italian-born court composer and Mozart's rival, Antonio Salieri, later lost his position and died half-crazy. On weak evidence he was rumored to have poisoned Mozart.

simplicity, except for some first movement refinements, kept it popular into the present century to the disadvantage of better works. "The public has long ears," Mozart said at one time, "politely" comparing his audience to donkeys.

What Fools These Mortals Be

Mozart's composition of the clever, worldly opera *Cosi fan Tutte* earlier that year brightened a dull period. His old partner Da Ponte collaborated on a story that Joseph II may have recommended as an exposé of the state of morals in Austria and may have been based on a real event.

The title page for a piano reduction of Cosi fan Tutte *depicts the two ladies trying to revive their "poisoned" suitors. In this pre-phonograph era, piano arrangements allowed music-lovers to enjoy opera in their homes.*

Its action stems from a wager made between two young officers and their bachelor drinking buddy that their fiancées are utterly true and faithful. The drinking buddy, Don Alfonso, laughs at the idea. Knowing women, he claims, he will surely win the bet. As a test, the two men pretend to go off to war but sneak back in Albanian disguise to woo each other's lady. They declare love at first sight, then gulp imaginary poison when the women reject them.

The maid Despina helps this plot along. Disguised as a quack doctor, she pulls the lethal doses from their bodies with an enormous magnet. (Theatergoers appreciated this jibe at a real-life personage, Dr. Mesmer, who worked with magnets.) So the "Albanians" recover and renew their courtship until the ladies' former loyalties crumble, though not without many tears, as they agree to marry these newcomers. Though the men have lost their bet, they have the satisfaction of returning in proper uniforms to confront their fiancées. Asking pardon, the embarrassed women renew pledges to their original mates.

Or do they? An alert director could match them to the new partners instead of the expected pairing. Or imply that the ladies saw through the game and tricked the very men hoping to trap *them*. In other words, the unfaithfulness could cut both ways. "That's what they all do."

With all its humor and superb music, *Cosi* ran into bad luck when Joseph II died. Vienna went into official mourning, and the entertainment industry faced hard times.

Continued misfortune dogged this opera. The prudish Beethoven admired *Cosi*'s score but not its intrigue. As a man whose idealism sometimes interfered with his sense of fun, he had condemned *Figaro* on the same grounds and resolved in his own opera *Fidelio* to celebrate married love, not hanky-panky. Enough others felt the same way to banish the work from most stages until it was resurrected in our own times. To modernize it, the first scene might take place in a health club, and the basic set for a TV production could be Despina's Diner—a greasy spoon somewhere in New Jersey. Or Kansas, or anywhere familiar.

But the implications are not obvious. In fact, *Cosi* becomes a favorite for people who know the tradition behind it. Elaborate arias burlesque, or mock, the warblings of

A page from Mozart's manuscript of orchestral and vocal parts in a Cosi fan Tutte *ensemble.*

leather-lunged sopranos. Masks and disguises are so improbable that we doubt that anybody's being fooled who doesn't want to be. We can't distinguish between the characters' real and simulated responses. In spite of several lyrical moments, such as the water music serenade over a delicious woodwind accompaniment early in act 2, the overall mood is summed up by a motto first heard in the overture. Later on, our three disillusioned males repeat it:

THE LAST YEARS ■ 77

This oddball opera furnishes lots of laughs. But it isn't indecent, and when heard a second time, not at all trivial. Mozart and Da Ponte dramatized the painful, wonderful urge to love—to love even the wrong person against better judgment. *Amor vincit omnium,* the old Latin phrase tells us: "love conquers all." What better slogan for a war-torn century?

New Projects

Mozart's next major project began when he picked up the libretto for *Die Zauberflöte,* or *The Magic Flute,* by theater owner, Freemason, and comic baritone Emanuel Schikaneder, whom he'd met long ago in Salzburg. This wheeler-dealer's suburban stage offered quite different fare from government-endorsed opera seria in Vienna proper. Though some people called Schikaneder's theater a big barn, it was capable of elaborate stage effects for magic operas and the like. Since its middle- and working-class customers didn't know or like Italian, plain, homespun German was preferred. Between songs, spoken dialogue or humorous patter (sometimes ad-lib, or spontaneous) replaced sung recitatives; thus acting prowess was as important then as it is today in Broadway musicals. Fairy operas were especially popular. The *Flute* promised to follow this trend.

Mozart interrupted work to head for his beloved Prague, this time to write and rehearse a new opera for the state visit of Leopold II in September. He was forced to use an ancient libretto by Metastasio, *The Clemency of Titus*—no longer the composer's cup of tea. The opera was to be finished within three weeks, and Mozart was helped by the loyal but uninspired assistant Süssmayr, who copied parts and wrote the recitatives. Mozart, meanwhile, felt ill and overworked and took medicines throughout his stay. In fact, all through his life, Mozart's childhood illnesses haunted him in the form of occasional fevers and fatigues.

Titus harked back to the old *Idomeneo,* though artistically inferior. Its message was the old one of charity and forgiveness in rulers, perhaps as a hint to the new emperor sitting among his Bohemian subjects. While some of them applauded, a certain lady of the royal party called it a beastly bore.

What could one expect from classic Roman sets and a stage full of people in togas? Also, Mozart scarcely had time to get it written down, much less to compose it with care. Modern audiences find *Titus* the least attractive of all his major works;

Singer and impresario Emanuel Schikaneder (1751–1812) was the chief librettist for Mozart's The Magic Flute *in 1791.*

The elaborate Roman stage setting for a Frankfurt production of The Clemency of Titus, *produced several years after Mozart's death.*

and a respected British commentator once argued that *"La Clemenza di Tito* [the original title] is an old-fashioned *opera seria* which was [already] a museum piece when it was written."[34]

Returning to the *Flute* in Vienna after this command performance must have been a relief. Always that summer he longed for Constanza, who was at Baden again for the cures. One of his letters suggested taking a certain medicine "rather than brandy." Did he fear she was enjoying herself too much? And were the dour descriptions of his own routine a cover-up for carousing with Schikaneder, whose borrowed summer house he worked in?

Weisheit, Vernuft, and Natur

Mozart's last opera is guided by three key words: *Weisheit, Vernuft,* and *Natur* (Wisdom, Reason, and Nature). Though many details are still mystifying, a scenario that moves from horseplay to serious philosophy and back again shouldn't dismay lovers of Dickens or Shakespeare, artists of similar range. In the imagination of all three, multilevel "sandwich" plots merge the highs and lows of human behavior. Real life shows the same mixture, but we expect art to be neater.

More on this in due time. The real authorship of the *Flute*'s libretto is still unsure.

Although Schikaneder is most likely, a certain Karl Ludwig Gieseke also figures in the picture. Since he advanced his claims in a tavern long afterward, however, few believed him then or now. Schikaneder must have written most, if not all, of the script. Mozart certainly lent a hand from start to finish. We know how closely he had worked with librettists on earlier jobs. The real issue is not who wrote what, but what this patchwork scenario adds up to.

The Magic Flute's plot goes like this: While traveling in a strange country, the prince Tamino is rescued from a serpent by three ladies dressed in black and carrying spears. They persuade him to come to the aid of their queen, whose daughter Pamina has been kidnapped by a sorcerer named Sarastro, the leader of a cult of priests. Amid thunder and lightning this Queen of the Night adds her own plea. Tamino is joined by the comic Papageno, a bird catcher wearing a suit of feathers and toting a cage on his back for specimens. Though cowardly at heart, he likes to brag.

The ladies padlock Papageno's lips for telling lies. Then they relent and give Tamino a flute and the birdman magic bells to ward off the perils of Sarastro's temple. When sent ahead to scout the way, Papageno finds the abducted maiden Pamina in the clutches of a wicked Moor who claims to be her guardian. As the latter flees the sight of the feathered human, Papageno and Pamina sing a duet in praise of marriage. While the womanless bird catcher longs for wedded bliss, innocent Pamina knows love only by hearsay. She is overjoyed to learn that a handsome prince intends to rescue her.

Meanwhile, Tamino approaches the temple, only to be halted by a priest at the gates of Wisdom, Reason, and Nature (the triple Masonic slogan). A dialogue with this official convinces the prince of Sarastro's

Prince Tamino (left), bird catcher Papageno (right), and the three ladies all eye the slain serpent at their feet. This engraving is part of a set probably based on the premiere of The Magic Flute *at Schikaneder's theater.*

Until now Tamino has known Pamina only through the portrait given him by the wily queen's forces. At the end of act 1, these two young people meet face-to-face inside the temple under Sarastro's kindly gaze. Tests and trials for both of them lie ahead.

A solemn march of the priests opens act 2. (It was evidently the last portion composed, written on the eve of the first performance. Nobody could work better under pressure than Mozart!) When a lesser priest asks if the convert will prove strong and brave, "for after all, he is a prince. . ." Sarastro's reply shows the new spirit of equality: "Even better, he is a *man*."

The other priests agree. Trials of blindfold, fasting, and silence follow. All-too-average Papageno is incapable of heroism. Thunder scares him; he shrinks from magic animals that Tamino confronts bravely. Spurned by her beloved, Pamina interprets his silence as rejection. As she is about to stab herself, the three genies (boy sopranos floating overhead) reason with her: Tamino is acting under orders; soon he will be free to join her.

As Papageno despairs of finding a mate, the birdwoman Papagena appears suddenly to tease him in an ugly-old-crone disguise. Then he too contemplates suicide, until the genies remind him of those magic bells. Their chimes summon his bride-to-be as a lovely nineteen-year-old. They express mutual surprise in the stammering duet "Pa-pa-pa-pa-papageno." True love throws them into each other's arms, and they discuss a future of many little Papagenos and Papagenas.

(Program notes from an old Deutsche Grammophone recording describe the two creators at work on this song: "Mozart

Papageno as performed by Schikaneder, from the playbill for the first performance.

virtue. For her own good, Pamina has been taken from an evil mother who personifies tyranny and superstition.

So informed, Tamino seems ready for induction into the brotherhood, provided he can survive initiation rites that seem to blend the Egyptian worship of Isis and Osiris with eighteenth century humanism. (Surely some of Mozart's audience missed this level of meaning, just as unsophisticated spectators at the Globe Theater ignored Shakespeare's soliloquies but loved swordfights.)

The awe-inspiring Queen of the Night appears amid moon and stars in this design from a nineteenth-century production of The Magic Flute.

at first composed the scene where Papageno and Papagena see each other for the first time quite differently. They were to see each other and cry 'Papageno!' 'Papagena!' But when Schikaneder heard this, he called out into the orchestra pit, 'Here, Mozart! This is no good—the music must show more amazement. We must both gaze dumbly at each other, and then Papageno must begin to stutter Pa-papapa-pa-pa; and Papagena must repeat it, until eventually we are both saying the whole name together.' Mozart fell in with this idea, and thus was born one of the most charming scenes in the opera.")[35]

The more dignified Tamino and Pamina enter gates of fire and water, and they are protected by the flute, which, as we now learn, was once carved from a sacred oak by the girl's late father. Thus it was *not* a token from the evil queen. After passing through these new threats (dangerous only for cowards, not the brave), they will become future leaders of Sarastro's realm. This hint of gender equality—possibly Mozart's idea more than his partner's—offsets earlier sexist wisecracks by some of the less enlightened priests.

The baffled queen and her cohorts storm Sarastro's temple but are thrust back into the darkness they deserve. Their downfall symbolizes a hoped-for end to political and religious repression. Tamino and Pamina ascend to their thrones. Sarastro yields power to them, and everyone rejoices at the victory of Truth over Falsehood.

A Bird Catcher and a High Priest

The *Flute* is a smorgasbord of simple folk songs, grand finales, and tunes like Papageno's entrance aria, which is punctuated by toots from his panpipes:

In contrast, Sarastro's prayer could belong in a Christian mass except for the invocation of pagan deities. George Bernard Shaw called it the only music good enough to be sung by God:

Both Schikaneder's and later productions included many theatrical gimmicks. Rabbits and monkeys cavorted to the sound of Tamino's flute; lions (or men in lion costumes) pulled Sarastro's chariot and later frightened Papageno into better behavior. Raging torrents and rocky, flame-lit caverns tested the lovers' stamina; the queen soared aloft on a throne among the moon and stars.

Unfortunately, many nineteenth century performances on both sides of the Atlantic overdid such effects. For a long while the plot seemed grade-schoolish, the morality so trite that only elaborate staging could save the piece. But at Weimar the poet-playwright Goethe had already produced it and even planned a sequel. According to him, any idiot could ridicule the *Flute*; rare intelligence was needed to understand it.

Now this opera endures as a timeless affirmation of wisdom, charity, and brotherhood—or, since Pamina achieves equal rank with her consort, the unity of all humankind, even the earthy bird catcher and his fertile frau. Without such values our world would revert to sterility and hatred.

Chapter 7 Who Murdered Mozart?

Mozart conducted the first two evenings of *The Magic Flute* at Emanuel Schikaneder's "off-Broadway" theater and attended other performances. One night he called in a carriage for Antonio Salieri and Salieri's mistress. This old competitor complimented the production warmly. Also it's recorded that Mozart stole backstage to play the glockenspiel (metal instrument played with hammers) accompaniment to a Schikaneder solo. He played it again when it was inappropriate, whereupon the unflappable Papageno told those bells to "shut up."

Not terribly popular at first, the opera's reputation continued to improve. Between 1791 and the 1850s it would be performed more than two hundred times on Schikaneder's stage alone. However, we don't know how the profits were shared.

And there were other events, happy and unhappy, that rocked Mozart's household. In late July 1791, just before Wolfgang left for Prague, Constanza gave birth to a healthy son, Franz Xaver, who later enjoyed a moderately successful musical career, though he was not a second Wolfgang. On the other hand, an anonymous, mysterious messenger called one night to order a requiem mass, and then turned up later to ask how it was progressing.

These visits haunted Mozart. He worried that the mass was for *him* and that the stranger was a ghost, an emissary from another world. (Only after his death was the identity of the messenger revealed as an employee of a certain Count Walsegg, who wished to memorialize a dead wife. But because Walsegg wanted to palm off Mozart's music as his own, he did not reveal his identity to the composer.) But once his *Magic Flute* was launched, Mozart worked frantically

Franz Xaver, the Mozarts' younger surviving son, as an adult.

Another Love Letter

Wolfgang, in Vienna, writes to Constanza at Baden on July 7, 1791. This excerpt is quoted from Emily Anderson's book:

"You cannot imagine how I have been aching for you all this long while. I can't describe what I have been feeling—a kind of emptiness, which hurts me dreadfully—a kind of longing, which is never satisfied, which never ceases, and which persists, nay rather increases daily. When I think how merry we were together at Baden—like children—and what sad, weary hours I am spending here! Even my work gives me no pleasure, because I am accustomed to stop working now and then and exchange a few words with you. Alas! this pleasure is no longer possible. If I go to the piano and sing something out of my opera, I have to stop at once, for this stirs my emotions too deeply."

The widowed Constanza some years after Wolfgang's death.

---

at the requiem's score for soloists, full orchestra, and chorus until Constanza sometimes took it away, fearing for her husband's sanity.

And why the strain? Because it was a death mass. After an initial *requiem aeternam,* or "rest eternal," and the usual *kyrie eleison,* or "Lord, have mercy," came a violent *dies irae* (day of wrath), along with other sequences alluding to "piercing flames," "a day of tears," and "the deep pit of Hell." Only toward the end could a familiar *benedictus* (benediction) and *agnus dei* (a prayer for peace) convey hope.

This was a heavy burden for an exhausted man subject to fears that undercut the good cheer—and Masonic optimism— of his new opera. The composition's mood more closely resembled that of Don Giovanni's damnation. Yet he stuck to the task. At last, late in November, fever and swelling of his limbs forced Mozart to bed, though he continued to instruct his scribe Süssmayr and to test finished portions aloud. With Constanza's authorization, the assistant promised to complete this project, as the Mozarts badly needed the money its sale would bring.

Since Mozart's handwriting extends only into the *lacrymosa*—halfway through the full score—Süssmayr's contributions are anybody's guess. At the end of the mass and aware of his own limitation, this faithful drudge reused materials from the opener, including a reverent double cadence of voices that prays for everlasting rest—and terminates in a Handel-style fugue with the words *cum sanctis tuis in aeternam*, "with thy saints for all eternity."

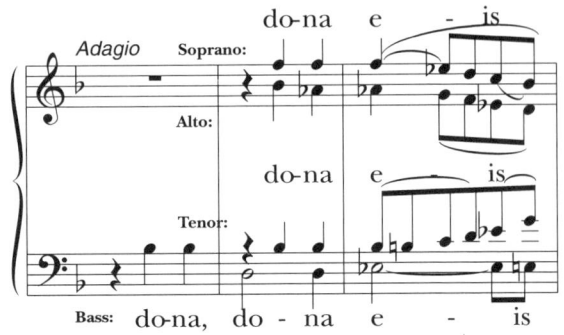

A Mysterious Letter

Erich Schenk's Mozart and His Time *quotes this letter, originally in Italian, supposedly from Mozart to Da Ponte in response to the latter's suggestion that they visit England together. Modern scholars consider it a forgery, even though the sentiments plausibly reflect Mozart's state of mind while composing the* Requiem:

"My very dear Sir!

I should like to follow your advice, but how can I do so? My head is confused; I can think only with difficulty and cannot free my mind of the image of the Unknown. I constantly see him before me; he pleads with me, presses me, and impatiently demands the work from me. I am continuing with it because the composing is less tiring than doing nothing. Besides, I have nothing more to fear. I can feel from my present state that the hour is striking. I am on the point of expiring. My end has come before I was able to profit by my talent. And yet life has been so beautiful, my career began under such fortunate auspices. But no one can change his fate. No one can count his days; one must resign oneself. What Providence determines will be done. I close now. Before me lies my swan song. I must not leave it incomplete.
Vienna, September 1791   Mozart"

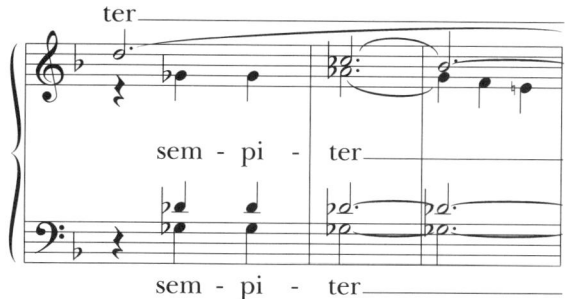

Whatever its clouded history, the *Requiem* ranks among Mozart's masterpieces. Only an unfinished earlier mass in C minor, written after his wedding, comes close. Either poor Süssmayr outdid himself, or Mozart's instructions for missing portions were more adequate than supposed. Only Bach's B Minor Mass, two or three of Haydn's works, Beethoven's almost unsingable *Missa Solemnis,* and Brahms's *German Requiem* belong in the same league. And the latter two might never have been written without Mozart as an inspiration.

Foul Play or Natural Death?

For two weeks Mozart lay bedridden, his fever and swelling gradually worsening. Two of Vienna's top physicians did more harm than good by bleeding Mozart's already frail body, using the standard medical practice of their profession. Instead of removing supposed impurities, this bloodletting further reduced vitality. The quack doctor in *Cosi fan Tutte* could have done a better job!

Bedside diagnoses and later speculations disagree on just what Mozart's ailments were. The best guess today seems to be endocarditis (internal heart infection, possibly affecting the valves) stemming from the rheumatic fever he had suffered as a child. Other hypotheses pinpoint kidney failure, venereal disease (now totally discounted), brain fever (a catchall term), and—notoriously—poisoning.

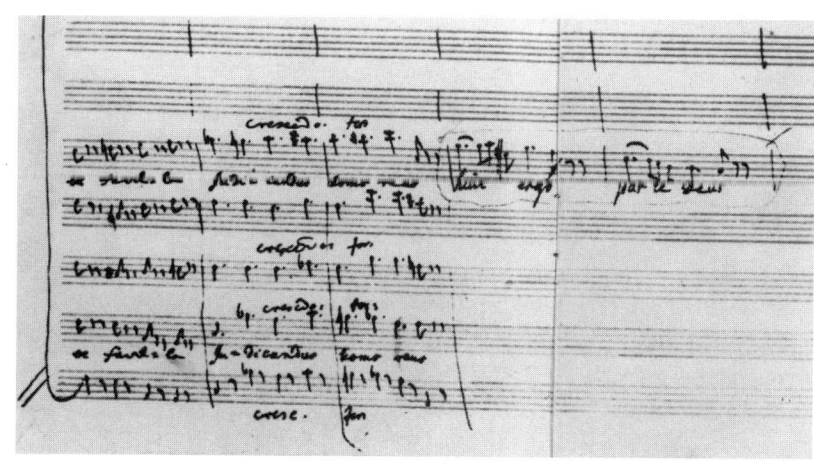

Mozart's sketch for the Lacrymosa of the Requiem, *the last notes from his hand before his death. The final two measures were added by an assistant.*

> ## An "Irreplaceable Loss"
>
> *Volkmar Braunbehrens's* Mozart in Vienna *quotes a newspaper's death notice as evidence of Mozart's excellent reputation:*
>
> "The Royal and Imperial Kammerkompositeur Wolfgang Amadeus Mozart died during the night of December 4–5. From childhood on he was known throughout Europe for his most exceptional musical talent. Through the successful development and diligent application of his extraordinary natural gifts, he scaled the heights of the greatest masters. His works, which are loved and admired everywhere, are proof of his greatness—and they reveal the irreplaceable loss which the noble art of music has suffered through his death."

Many amateur sleuths have considered the poison theory, and some believe it. Constanza recalled Mozart's fear that an unknown enemy had fed him a dose of *aqua toffana*—a blend of arsenic, lead, and antimony (a metallic element) that could be slipped unnoticed into coffee or food. It would produce slow-working but fatal effects.

Mozart felt enormous emotional pressures at the time, and his obsession with *The Requiem* disturbed his mental balance. Also, Constanza's reminiscences long after the fact may not be trustworthy. At the time she paid no attention to rumors of murder.

If a Murder, Whodunit?

If it was murder, the question remains as to who would have perpetrated it. One theory targets the Freemasons, who were supposedly angry at Mozart for revealing lodge secrets in *The Magic Flute*. According

In this sentimental rendition completed long after the event, a dying Mozart rehearses his Requiem *with friends. Constanza leans over his shoulder; her younger sister Sophie is at the keyboard.*

A Crazy Plot

The scholar Edward J. Dent describes in Mozart's Operas *the starting point for Schikaneder's "fairytale plot." Other authorities take the libretto much more seriously.*

"The libretto of Die Zauberflöte has generally been considered to be one of the most absurd specimens of that form of literature in which absurdity is regarded as a matter of course. What Schikaneder wanted was a fairytale plot of the conventional kind—a good fairy, a wicked magician, a pair of lovers passing through various trials and ultimately united, thanks to the virtues of a musical instrument endowed with magic properties; the scene was to be laid in . . . 'the East'; there were to be startling scenic effects, with plenty of coloured fire and plenty of animals; the actor-manager himself was to have a comic part full of popular songs."

Another artist's version of Papageno with bird cage and panpipes.

to this theory, they administered poison and then arranged their victim's speedy burial, without autopsy, in an unmarked grave. But if that were the case, why did Schikaneder go unpunished by the organization for his role in writing the opera? Moreover, the fanfare in E-flat, the grand master role of Sarastro, and the initiation rite were known publicly. No official rituals or symbols that were not already public knowledge had been leaked by Mozart.

Furthermore, Masonic power had shrunk since the mid-1780s. Tolerance gave way to suspicion, and lodge members were considered political liabilities. Before his death, Joseph II had restricted their powers. Rather than divulging secrets, the *Flute* may actually have been a last-ditch effort to restore the organization's prestige.

Another possible culprit was Mozart's old rival Salieri, for years a kingpin of Vienna's musical establishment. His motive would have been envy. Gossip then and afterward mentioned him as the most likely suspect—but why? This favorite of the emperors had little to fear politically or financially from his rival. Constanza felt good enough about the alleged villain to employ him later for her young son's music lessons.

Years later in failing health and in old age Salieri may actually have confessed, rather than denied, his guilt. At least he felt some sort of generalized responsibility, active or passive, for the Mozart tragedy. But even this assumption rests on flimsy evidence. A Leipzig newspaper tried to set the record straight:

> Our worthy Salieri, to use the popular phrase, just can't die. His body suffers all the pains of infirm old age, and his mind is gone. In the frenzy of his imagination he is even said to accuse himself of complicity in Mozart's early death: a rambling of the mind believed in truth by no one other than the poor deluded old man himself. To Mozart's contemporaries it is unfortunately all too well known that only over-exertion at his work, and fast living in ill-chosen company, shortened his precious days![36]

This report spread rumors rather than settling them. Certainly the film *Amadeus*, like the stage play of the same name, made too much of the composers' relationship. Its film-script even portrayed the older man posing as that mysterious stranger who ordered *The Requiem* after having done his utmost to block earlier opportunities for the young genius—slight truth in that. And Salieri certainly did not sit at Mozart's bedside helping to copy the mass—a total fabrication.

Conspiracy theories are impossible to quash once they circulate. Familiar to us are the conflicting accounts of President John F. Kennedy's death or Elvis's reappearances. In the Mozart mystery, still another scenario accuses a public official named Hofdemel of the dirty work as revenge for his wife's supposed intimacy with Mozart while she was a piano pupil. Though the story was doubted at the time, those who advance it now—especially Francis Carr in *Mozart and Constanza*—allege a cover-up, again by Freemasons, to keep Mozart's name free of scandal. It is true that Hofdemel attacked his wife with a razor on the day after Mozart's death and then cut his own throat with the same weapon, but the timing could have been coincidental. Domestic violence has many possible triggers.

The aging Salieri, sometime after Mozart's death.

Mozart died in this house (left of center) on December 5, 1791.

Constanza's Role

Other arguable issues surround Mozart's death. An often repeated one is that Constanza did not grieve her husband's death. She has been labeled an insensitive and even unfaithful spouse: unmusical, unaware of her husband's gifts, a bad mother and worse homemaker, a malingerer, and a compulsive shopper. Also, she is accused of taking his death too calmly. Besides, she remarried (and why not, almost twenty years later?), this time to a Danish diplomat, and lived to a comfortable old age.

However, she took good care of Mozart's manuscripts and even undertook performances of his work. We know that she was a capable singer and liked fugues. Also, she and her second husband, Georg Nissen, prepared the first reliable Mozart biography. At the time of Wolfgang's death she had been too distraught to attend the funeral or observe cemetery rites. Also, the weather may have been awful, especially for a woman in uncertain health.

Another long-held belief is that Mozart died an unknown, unrecognized pauper. Though the body was tumbled into a raw grave, these descriptions of a pauper's burial are grossly distorted. We should remember that Joseph II had pronounced edicts against lavish funeral displays. Probably Mozart's lodge brothers, and especially his old patron Baron van Swieten, came to the widow's aid by following the late emperor's recommendations for a plain coffin or shroud, quicklime to kill bacteria and hasten decomposition, and a nameless trench. This procedure would also save money. Notices in the papers and talk around town showed no lack of respect for the late composer, even though his last years deserved better financial support.

Sophie's Story

Constanza's younger sister, Sophie Weber Haibl, sent a classic description of Mozart's last hours to Constanza's second husband when the composer's biography was being prepared in 1825. No doubt she wanted to be as accurate as the passage of time permitted.

She mentioned improved relations between Mozart and his mother-in-law, to whom he often brought gifts of coffee and sugar. As his illness turned critical, mother and daughter sewed a nightshirt to be put on from the front, now that he was too swollen to roll over easily in bed. He appreciated both this present and a quilted nightgown, and for a while seemed to improve, so Sophie decided to skip her customary daily visit to Constanza and Wolfgang.

But that evening as she was lighting a candle, the flame went out mysteriously. Fearing an omen, she told Frau Weber what had happened, and her mother urged her to check up on the invalid immediately.

At the Mozarts', Sophie found Constanza "half demented yet trying to control herself." Wolfgang had seemed near death the night before, and he might not last another evening. But from his bed the sick man thanked his sister-in-law for coming. "You must stay here tonight, you must watch me die," he said. "I have the taste of death on my tongue already."

Sophie ran home with this news, stopping on the way to get a reluctant priest (because of Mozart's lodge membership), and returned to find Süssmayr in the composer's bedroom. From this point her own words speak eloquently:

> The well-known Requiem lay on the coverlet, and Mozart was explaining to him how he thought he should finish it after his death.... There was a long search for Glosett, the doctor, who was found in the theater; but he had to wait till the play was over—then he came and prescribed *cold* compresses on his burning head, and these gave him such a shock that he did not regain

Another melodramatic version of the dying Mozart, at work on his Requiem *while Constanza tries to comfort him.*

consciousness before he passed away. The last thing he did was to try and mouth the sound of the tympani in his Requiem; I can still hear it now.... Dear brother[-in-law], I cannot possibly describe the boundless misery of his faithful wife as she threw herself on her knees and implored succour from the Almighty. She could not tear herself from him, beg her as I did; if her grief had been susceptible of increase it must have increased on the day after that dreadful night by people passing by in crowds, lamenting and weeping for him loudly.[37]

Sophie also wrote that Mozart was never impatient during his illness and that his hearing was still so sensitive that they removed a pet canary from his room because it excited him too much.

Nowhere in her story is poison mentioned. Her grief and Constanza's were profound, but in the true spirit of the man's *Requiem,* neither of them dishonored the event with unjust suspicions.

In Memoriam

Whatever else is known or guessed, all traces of the composer's body and his grave are lost, in spite of recent claims of his skull having been discovered. Maybe that is best. It can be said of Wolfgang Amadeus Mozart, as Ben Jonson said after the death of Shakespeare, that "he was not of an age, but for all time."

Another dominant intellect of that era was Sir Christopher Wren, architect of St. Paul's Cathedral in London—a building Mozart had surely seen in his youth. Wren ordered this epitaph for a slab under its dome:

SI MONUMENTUM REQUIRIS, CIRCUMSPICE

"If you seek [my] monument, look around you." If seeking Mozart's monument, open your ears to any of his more than six hundred works, several of which are certainly being played or sung or whistled somewhere around the world at this very moment.

Chapter 8
Mozart Then and Now

Though he was honored, but not fully supported, in his own time, Mozart's status as a supreme artist slowly grew, helped along by the understanding of such equals and near equals as Beethoven, Schubert, and Mendelssohn. Even opera composer Verdi, a different sort of musician, paid the compliment of sneaking a minuet into the first act of *Rigoletto*, in the manner of Mozart's interlude in *Don Giovanni*. Wagner also revered the earlier master, learning more from Mozart's *Magic Flute* than he liked to admit.

Nineteenth-century musical taste—often vulgarized by the new "star" system, by sentiment and melodrama and fussy Victorian prudery, and by low standards of performance and musical scholarship—at least kept the major Mozart symphonies and concertos alive and, in time, gathered enough of the scattered Mozart lore to produce reputable biographies.

Though his mature operas achieved early and wide popularity, they suffered from insensitive criticism and unwise alterations. *Don Giovanni*, for example, reached the city of Leipzig within a year of its composition, and Mainz shortly after, but translated into German from the original Italian. Munich banned it temporarily, because of either the scandalous plot or the title character's impiety. Late in life Da Ponte arranged for its performance in New York City, where he had ended up as a language teacher. The quality was poor. And the Parisian version in 1834 added crowd scenes, ballets, and passages from the *Requiem* to accompany Giovanni into hell. Also, some non-Mozart music was introduced. In Russia, Giovanni became a tenor, and poor Don Ottavio a soprano!

Still another idealized posthumous portrait of the composer.

> ### Don Giovanni as Hero, not Villain
>
> *In* Mozart: The Man and His Work, *W. J. Turner quotes Soren Kierkegaard on the subject of Don Juan (Giovanni) as a symbol of the Life Force:*
>
> "If I conceive Don Juan musically [rather than realistically] I then have before me the power of nature, the demonic, which never wearies of seducing, which never stops—as little as the wind stops blowing, the sea rolling. . . .
>
> The power of desire never grows weak and only when he [Don Juan] desires is he in his right element. There he sits spreading joy like a god and drains the goblet, jumps up, napkin in hand, and is ready for the onslaught . . . his life foams and bubbles like the wine with which he refreshes himself."

Even so, tampering was better than total neglect. Some of the public still thought of Mozart as salon entertainment; others felt he merely set the table for Beethoven's bigger musical feasts. When Mozart's sometimes bawdy notes to his cousin Bäsle were publicized, still other people took offense. For such folks Dyneley Hussey offered good advice:

> Mozart was intensely serious about everything that really mattered. And music always mattered most. Even as a child he wrote with the utmost gravity about the performances he heard in Italy; and, when he grew up, religion, in the widest sense, and the broad issues of moral conduct always evoked from him an earnest expression of his convictions, which is at times tinged with youthful priggishness. This fundamental seriousness in his character prevented him from indulging in his music the vulgar fun which sometimes shocks readers of his letters.[38]

Slowly he became a demigod for those who best knew his works. The French composer Gounod applied such terms as "divine" and "perfect beauty" and "complete humanity with the simplicity of a child."[39] Instead of dismissing Mozart as superficial and "pretty," the Romantic author and composer E. T. A. Hoffman said that the man "strives for the superhuman and the miraculous that dwells in the depths of the mind." Thus his music becomes "the mysterious language of a distant spiritual kingdom, whose marvelous accents echo in our inner being and arouse a higher, intensive life."[40]

This may sound like modern advertising hype, but Hoffman spoke from the heart. And the Danish philosopher Kierkegaard was profoundly moved by the problem of evil in the rakish Don Giovanni. As a Christian he condemned; as an existentialist he admitted that a genuine spiritual life could not be founded on comfortable habits alone. Moral choices must be faced.

Even in distant Russia the nineteenth-century poet Pushkin knew enough of the legend of Mozart to write a brief drama about Mozart and Salieri—one of the predecessors to Hollywood's *Amadeus* in our own time.

At the turn of the century, George Bernard Shaw, a music critic and competent pianist before he turned playwright, felt utmost respect for Mozart, despite his own preference for realism, social reform, and the gigantic music dramas of Wagner. Many others concurred. We can now attend authentic productions of *Figaro* and *Don Giovanni,* all the way from the annual music festivals in Salzburg or Glyndebourne in England, to New York and Chicago and San Francisco and Rio de Janeiro in the New World, and to the exotic harbor-front opera house in Sydney, Australia, halfway around the earth.

Moreover, symphony orchestras could not exist without the works of Haydn, Mozart, Beethoven, and Brahms at the core of their repertoires. The same holds true for chamber music groups. Great conductors, from Toscanini and Furtwängler to Von Karajan, Solti, and Bernstein, have interpreted those masters of orchestral music very differently. Their renditions are known to millions through recordings and tapes.

At the same time, scholars have corrected old scores and revived old instruments and styles of performance. So many biographies and studies have tumbled from the presses that libraries contain whole shelves of Mozart materials, ranging from popularized to highly technical.

The dead genius from Salzburg is here to stay. So much so that he may suffer from excess popularity, as Ottaway warned a decade ago:

> Advantages, it is said, carry disadvantages on their backs, and in one sense this may well be applicable to Mozart and ourselves. It concerns the problem of over-familiarity. Performances of some of Mozart's greatest works—the last three symphonies, for instance—have become so "everyday" that, as listeners, we may easily slip into a too-familiar response. We are lulled by the certainty of what comes next and our listening ceases to be active. The best corrective is to widen our scope, to make a point of experiencing some of the unfamiliar works. These, in turn, will provide fresh insights.[41]

The baritone Francisco d'Andrade (1859–1921) sings Giovanni's champagne aria as he invites guests to a feast and dance at his palace.

A Balanced View of Mozart

In Mozart and His Piano Concertos, *the British mathematician and part-time musicologist C. W. Girdlestone accounts for the composer's universal appeal:*

"The revival of Mozart since the opening of the [twentieth] century is one form of the reaction against Romanticism. Yet he is not the 'pure' musician, untainted by emotion, whom some thought they saw in him twenty years ago.... We have come to love in him one of the healthiest and most imaginative natures in all art. He is discreet, not because he has nothing to say, but because he speaks with a moderation and a sense of form that few artists have so consistently exhibited. Let us no longer judge him from his minor works, sonatas or trios. His true face is shown in his best quartets and quintets, his last symphonies and his Viennese concertos, his operas, his C minor and *Requiem* masses. There he throbs with as intense a life as Bach or Beethoven.... His inner life is of the richest and most communicative; his work, a personal revelation which never falls into a series of self-centered confessions. It is as much a testament as that of the greatest masters, capable of affording unfailing comfort and support."

The fact that Mozart's works remain some of the most performed pieces today is testimony to the appeal of this great artist's music across the generations.

Highbrow and Lowbrow

Few of us in modern America know Mozart that well. To some of us he is a nonentity or an old bore. To others, musical classics such as the *Jupiter* Symphony are works to admire or mention at parties, but not vital experiences.

In such cases the communication failure lies with us, not with the symphony. A barrage of cookie-cutter music on radio or record player or boom box discourages concentration on any of it. Only by paying close attention to the substance of good jazz or blues or the *Jupiter* and other compositions of its type do we begin to understand the conventions or rules of the game back then.

Football, soccer, and other complex field sports are also "classics" that must be studied to become meaningful for either players or passive spectators. Likewise, familiarity and close attention—especially if voluntary and enthusiastic, and *not* textbook-bound—leads us into seemingly difficult music of the past.

Often, people do not listen to Mozart because they feel his music is distant, elitist. Many people, both now and in previous centuries, attended concerts to show off fancy clothing, to meet friends, to flaunt social status, or to appear more cultured than their neighbors. But sheer love of music attracted the genuine listeners. Music enlarged their range of emotions, made them more fully human, added beauty and order to harrassed lives. Then, too, Mozart and Beethoven and the rest were not so highfalutin' as first appears. Often they adapted popular tunes; they spoke for ordinary women and men rather than cults; and perhaps more importantly, they invited participation. Mozart aimed a sizable portion of his output at amateurs: piano students, informal chamber music groups, and church choirs of good but not unusual ability; also at theaters of ordinary ticket buyers who wanted nice melodies and entertaining plots.

In fact, the man in the street remembered Mozart's best songs (as their composer bragged in Prague) and enjoyed these same materials recycled in piano and woodwind and even dance hall arrangements—just the way sheet music used to be enjoyed in the United States. What is the *Flute* but musical comedy, 1790s style? What are Figaro's and Papageno's songs but best-sellers in the making?

Mozart's monument in Vienna's Burggarten, erected in 1896.

These remarks are not meant to cheapen such music, nor to oversimplify a great artistic heritage, but only to point out its meaningfulness on several levels. It may not remake the world. We know that both Hitler and Göring loved the stuff. So did the great organist-doctor-missionary Albert Schweitzer. Thus music is not automatically moral or politically correct; it cannot cure violence between nations or within cities; and, like religion, it can serve good causes or bad. But we find music in every culture—although the forms differ tremendously—because humanity finds life empty without it.

This medium works not only superficially but deep-down "where the meanings are," as Emily Dickinson would say. At its greatest, music appeals to both the senses and the spirit. It is a pacifier in the fullest sense of the word. So argued the theologian Karl Barth, who began each day listening to Mozart on his record player, and only then turned to the newspapers or his scholarly books:

> [Mozart's music] is free of all exaggeration, of all sharp breaks and contradictions. The sun shines but does not blind, does not burn or consume. Heaven arches over the earth, but it does not weight it down, it does not crush or devour it. Hence earth remains earth, with no need to maintain itself in a titanic revolt against heaven. Granted, darkness, chaos, death and hell do appear, but not for a moment are they allowed to prevail. Knowing all, Mozart creates music from a mysterious center, and so knows and observes limits to the right and the left, above and below. He maintains moderation.[42]

Notes

Introduction: In Search of Mozart

1. Robert L. Marshall, *Mozart Speaks*. New York: Schirmer Books, 1991.
2. Marshall, *Mozart Speaks*.
3. Marshall, *Mozart Speaks*. (The translation retains the original verse form.)
4. Marshall, *Mozart Speaks*.
5. Emily Anderson, *The Letters of Mozart and His Family*. New York: W.W. Norton, 1985.

Chapter 1: Boy Wonder

6. Otto Eric Deutsch, *Mozart: A Documentary Biography*. Stanford, CA: Stanford University Press, 1966.
7. Deutsch, *Mozart: A Documentary Biography*.
8. Anderson, *The Letters of Mozart and His Family*.

Chapter 2: Toward Self-Knowledge

9. Rudolph Angermüller, *Mozart's Operas*. New York: Rizzoli, 1988.
10. Marshall, *Mozart Speaks*.
11. Anderson, *The Letters of Mozart and His Family*.
12. Anderson, *The Letters of Mozart and His Family*.
13. Hugh Ottaway, *Mozart*. Detroit: Wayne State University Press, 1980.
14. Anderson, *The Letters of Mozart and His Family*.
15. Anderson, *The Letters of Mozart and His Family*.

Chapter 3: A Changed Life in Changing Times

16. Edward Crankshaw, *Maria Theresa*. New York: Viking Press, 1970.
17. Crankshaw, *Maria Theresa*.
18. Crankshaw, *Maria Theresa*.
19. Kurt Frank Reinhardt, *Germany: 2000 Years, Vol. II*. New York: F. Ungar and Company, 1961.
20. John E. Rodes, *Germany: A History*. New York: Holt, Rinehart, and Winston, 1964.
21. Anderson, *The Letters of Mozart and His Family*.
22. Anderson, *The Letters of Mozart and His Family*.

Chapter 4: Boom Times

23. Anderson, *The Letters of Mozart and His Family*.
24. W. J. Turner, *Mozart: The Man and His Works*. New York: Tudor Publishing Company, 1938.
25. Anderson, *The Letters of Mozart and His Family*.
26. Anderson, *The Letters of Mozart and His Family*.
27. Deutsch, *Mozart: A Documentary Biography*.

Chapter 5: Good Luck and Bad

28. Ottaway, *Mozart*.
29. Anderson, *The Letters of Mozart and His Family*.
30. Stanley Sadie, *The New Grove Mozart*. New York: W. W. Norton, 1982.
31. Reported in many sources but not authenticated.
32. Anderson, *The Letters of Mozart and His Family*.

Chapter 6: The Last Years

33. Anderson, *The Letters of Mozart and His Family*.

34. Edward J. Dent, *Mozart's Operas: A Critical Study*. London: Oxford University Press, 1947.

35. Program notes for Deutsche Grammophone recording of *Die Zauberflöte,* conductor Karl Bohm with Berlin Philharmonic. This anecdote, though plausible, is doubted by many scholars.

Chapter 7: Who Murdered Mozart?

36. Deutsch, *Mozart: A Documentary Biography.*
37. Deutsch, *Mozart: A Documentary Biography.*

Chapter 8: Mozart Then and Now

38. Dyneley Hussey, *Wolfgang Amade Mozart*. New York: Harper and Brothers, 1928.
39. Hussey's title page quotes this in the original French. Translation by author.
40. Ottaway, *Mozart.*
41. Ottaway, *Mozart.*
42. Karl Barth, *Wolfgang Amadeus Mozart*. Grand Rapids, MI: William B. Eerdmans Publishing Company, 1986.

Glossary

baroque: A general term for styles in the arts from 1600 to the death of Bach in 1750. Church music, opera, and other forms are characterized by pomp, rich texture, and strong emotional thrust.

cadenza: A showy passage either written down or improvised at the end of a concerto movement. Mozart sometimes wrote his own, but performers can ad-lib. Though cadenzas can become tedious displays of muscular prowess, Mozart's and Beethoven's are tied to previous materials in the movement.

coloratura: A style marked by trills, runs, and other decorations to show off the singer's prowess (usually a soprano's).

concerto: The posing of a solo instrument—or set of instruments, as in Bach's *Brandenburg Concertos*—against the *tutti* or full ensemble. Mozart's *Sinfonia Concertante* is, in fact, a double concerto for violin, viola, and orchestra. He also wrote concertos for bassoon, oboe, flute, clarinet, two pianos, three pianos, and over two dozen for solo piano.

counterpoint: The art of setting two or more vocal or instrumental lines against each other. The old round "Row, row, row your boat..." is a familiar example. Fugues are more extended and obey certain strict rules. Depending on the composer's skills, fugues can employ four or more voices.

countertenor: An adult male voice able to sing at a soprano or near-soprano range.

divertimento: A suite of several movements for small orchestra or ensemble and designed for easy listening. Mozart used the term almost interchangeably with "serenade" and sometimes, as in the "Haffner Serenade" made it a much more serious musical statement.

fugue: from the Latin *fuga* or "flight." In music, a fugue is a disciplined interweave of a theme by a number of voices and/or instruments entering successively. At least in Baroque and Classical practice, fugues obeyed rather strict rules.

galant or galante: A Rococo style marked by decorativeness (often to an extreme) and by wispy sentimentality—as in some of Mozart's lighter chamber music and piano variations. The galant is not in good repute nowadays, but it was a natural expression of lighthearted aristocratic emotions.

harmony: The vertical element in music of simultaneous tones and series of tones forming stable or unstable chords. In classical practice harmony was stabilized in triads formed on each note of major and minor scales. Most important was the cadence from dominant back to tonic (that is, from G to C in the key of C). Harmony was enriched by incorporating inversions, sevenths, diminished sevenths, altered chords, and modulations into new keys until, with Schoenberg, avant garde practice virtually outmoded the old rules, though they survived in much popular music. Those interested should consult Walter Piston's *Harmony* or other standard texts.

K. numbers: Opus (publication) numbers were not yet common in Mozart's time. Key, or else genre number, identified symphonies and concertos. Mozart began cataloging his works in mid-career, and his list was incomplete. In the mid-nineteenth century Ludwig von Köchel inventoried Mozart's output in chronological order. With some alterations, this system is still used.

libretto: from the Latin for "little book." The words, as distinguished from the "score" or music, of an opera or oratorio. For shorter works such as songs, the term "text" is used.

The Mass: In Latin, and now in many languages, the Catholic sacrament of the body and blood of Christ. Parts or all may be spoken or chanted, but for High Mass, the "Ordinary"—the unchanging sections—can be set to music. The "Ordinary" usually comprises the Kyrie, Gloria, Credo, Sanctus, Benedictus, and Agnus Dei. A *Requiem* or Funeral Mass differs in several ways. After the "Requiem aeternam dona eis" (Lord, grant them eternal rest) comes a sequence that describes the Last Judgment. Sanctus, Benedictus, and an enlarged Agnus Dei (Lamb of God) complete the work.

Mozart composed masses in Salzburg, an incomplete C Minor Mass to celebrate his marriage, and the likewise unfinished *Requiem*. Shorter sacred works included vespers, motets, and quasi-religious pieces for the Masons.

motet: A short choral composition, usually to a religious text, and sung *a capella* (without orchestral accompaniment).

notation: Most familiar are the G clef and F clef sitting above and below middle C, respectively. Violas and other instruments may use a clef suitable to their range. Positions on the lines or spaces indicate pitch; shape of the notes or their stems and flags indicate duration. Guitar players know another system that represents the frets on their instrument. The advent of electronic music requires new methods, such as graphs and numerical formulas. At great savings of time and expense, computer printouts can now create scores that were once hand inscribed by composers or professional copyists.

Mozart's memory and improvising skill allowed him to perform, if he wished, using only a few memory aids, if not from total recall. Nowadays professional soloists usually perform from memory; choral and instrumental ensembles rely on the printed or manuscript page.

opera: A long dramatic work set to music. *Opera seria* for Mozart meant sung or chanted recitatives, formal arias, and plots from classic sources. The preferred language was Italian. *Opera buffa* moved more briskly, contained humor, and ended happily even if there were tense or serious moments meanwhile, as in *Don Giovanni*. The *singspiel* used spoken dialogue and slapstick, sometimes supernatural plots, songs and ensembles of a folklike simplicity, and German language. *The Magic Flute* is a shining example.

orchestra: For Mozart, strings, flutes, oboes, bassoons, and French horns were standard. Big effects called for trumpets and tympani, occasionally trombones. The clarinet came relatively late; basset horns were fading in popularity. The ensemble might number two dozen players or more, depending on the orchestra's finances. As a leftover from the past, some of Haydn's symphonies still called for a continuo keyboard part, but the sonorous quality of other instruments made the keyboard irrelevant, except when it starred in concertos.

recitative and aria: Recitative denotes an introduction, or filler between numbers, in normal speech, but with musical intonation, against either thin orchestra sound or harpischord accompaniment. Oddly enough, *opera seria* carried the action through recitatives, while arias depicted "frozen" emotion.

Old-fashioned arias were often *da capo*: repeating the first section, often more ornamented, after a middle section. Some Mozart arias fall into three parts, each faster and more excited than its predecessor. The simpler (but no less profound) *Magic Flute* contains songs or airs, often of repeated stanzas (as in Papageno's entrance number). The trend of nineteenth-century opera toward realism, or *verismo,* discredited old-fashioned separate arias until late Verdi, Wagner, and Puccini, among others, preferred a continuous flow from beginning to end. The aria format still prevails in Broadway musicals.

rococo: A lighthearted, less intellectual outgrowth of baroque associated with Marie Antoinette, wispy landscapes, and filigree ornamentation. Musical texture tends toward simpler structure but fancier details. Some of it, especially the so-called galant, seems artificial and frivolous now. Mozart could work his way into and out of rococo clichés with ease.

singspiel: Comic opera (*The Magic Flute* as a very complex example) sung in German, with spoken rather than sung recitatives and humorous dialogue. It can be termed an ancestor of modern musical comedy.

sonata form: A "floorplan" for movements in the classical vein. An exposition states main and subordinate themes, customarily ending on the dominant. Development plays with these materials or new ones, even adventuring into strange keys. The recapitulation repeats the exposition, often with new twists, and finally affirms, the original key the piece is written in. Sometimes a coda, topping off the movement, becomes a second brief development. A stately introduction to the first movement was optional. Sonata form as a design must not be confused with the sonata proper: a composition, usually in two or more movements, for solo or paired instruments.

Sturm und Drang: "Storm and Stress," a term for the pre-Romantic political and personal turmoil in mid- and late-eighteenth-century Germany. Schiller, early Goethe, and Haydn's choppy, angry, middle-period symphonies seem typical. Sturm und Drang is connected to the unrest and anxiety of a country emerging from outworn aristocratic and religious restrictions. Mozart used its wildness when convenient, as in the hellfire ending of *Don Giovanni,* but he was normally too disciplined for such extravagance.

symphony: A catchall term for extended compositions for large ensembles. The normal symphony in Mozart's time comprised a brisk first movement in sonata form, a slow second movement in modified sonata form or theme-and-variations, a dancelike third movement (minuet and trio), and a frisky last movement in sonata or rondo form.

Beethoven's minuet-and-trio movements became too rambunctious to even imply dancing. He preferred the term *scherzo*.

Smaller ensembles such as string quartets, piano trios, and also solo sonatas, also used the symphony layout. For social music (*divertimenti,* serenades, and so forth) Mozart often added minuets and other sections to the basic four-movement scheme.

tutti: from the Latin *tutus* meaning "all" or "complete." In music, a passage performed by the whole orchestra rather than soloists or a small ensemble.

tympani: Kettledrums (*Pauken* in German). Large cauldron-shaped metal drums with a drumhead on top. They come in several sizes and the pitch of each can be adjusted; thus (unlike snare- or bass-drums) they can conform to the harmonies of the score, as well as accenting climaxes.

For Further Reading

Emily Anderson, *The Letters of Mozart and His Family*, 3d ed. New York: W. W. Norton, 1985. The best and most complete collection in English translation, arranged chronologically.

Karl Barth, *Wolfgang Amadeus Mozart*. Grand Rapids, MI: William B. Eerdmans Publishing Company, 1986. This hard-to-find pamphlet contains an eminent modern theologian's thoughts about Mozart.

Marcia Davenport, *Mozart*. New York: Charles Scribner's Sons, 1932. Good reading, but a fictionalized account and often undependable.

Edward J. Dent, *Mozart's Operas: A Critical Study*. London: Oxford University Press, 1947. A classic treatment by a wise, witty scholar.

Robert Harris, *What to Listen for in Mozart*. New York: Simon and Schuster, 1991. A compact biography that includes basic musical analysis of major compositions.

Wolfgang Hildesheimer, *Mozart*. New York: Random House, 1982. Melodramatic and heavy on the "neglected genius" side, but a popular, influential biography.

H. C. Robbins Landon, *Mozart: The Golden Years*. New York: Schirmer Books, 1989. A foremost Haydn and Mozart scholar presents the latest findings about the successes and failures of Mozart's years in Vienna. Though Landon is a good writer, readers will face difficult material at times.

H. C. Robbins Landon, editor, *The Mozart Compendium*. New York: Schirmer Books, 1990. Now considered the definitive reference work, with articles by various authorities that cover Mozart's times, his biography, and a complete catalogue of the music that includes details of commissioning, first performance, publication, variants in manuscripts or editions, and so forth. Every Mozart-lover should know this book, not to read straight through, but to use as a "Mozart encyclopedia."

H. C. Robbins Landon, *Mozart's Last Year*. New York: Schirmer Books, 1988. A companion to the above-named *Golden Years*, equally important.

Robert L. Marshall, *Mozart Speaks*. New York: Schirmer Books, 1991. Passages from Mozart's correspondence arranged by topic, with explanatory notes.

Hugh Ottaway, *Mozart*. Detroit: Wayne State University Press, 1980. Probably the most user-friendly introduction to the composer's life and works, generously illustrated.

William Stafford, *The Mozart Myths*. Stanford, CA: Stanford University Press, 1992. As of this date the most recent survey of fact and fiction regarding the composer's death. After weighing evidence, Stafford is open-minded, yet wary of poison and conspiracy theories.

W. J. Turner, *Mozart: The Man and His Works*. New York: Tudor Publishing Company, 1938. An older but not outdated biography. Clear and helpful treatment of the composer's life and excellent analysis of the music, written in plain language.

Works Consulted

Rudolph Angermüller, *Mozart's Operas*. New York: Rizzoli, 1988. Sources, first productions, and stage histories of major and minor dramatic works, abundantly illustrated and indispensable for those interested in costumes, sets, and so forth.

Eric Blom, *Mozart*. London: J. M. Dent and Sons, 1935, 1962. An old-fashioned but readable example of British scholarship combining biography and musical analysis.

Peter Branscombe, *Die Zauberflöte*. Cambridge and London: Cambridge University Press, 1991. Detailed treatment of all aspects of *The Magic Flute*. See companion volumes of this series on the other major Mozart operas.

Volkmar Braunbehrens, *Mozart in Vienna*. New York: Grove Weidenfeld, 1986, 1989. Updated and balanced German scholarship covering not only the composer's last ten years, but also Austria's political and social situation during that time.

Francis Carr, *Mozart and Constanza*. New York: Franklin Watts, 1984. A gossipy mix of history and conjecture by an author inclined to doubt Constanza's and Wolfgang's faithfulness and to emphasize conspiracy theories about the latter's death.

Catherine Clement, *Opera, or the Undoing of Women*. Minneapolis: University of Minnesota Press, 1987. A feminist study of the fate of heroines in operas by Mozart, Verdi, and others.

Edward Crankshaw, *Maria Theresa*. New York: Viking Press, 1970. The best full biography of Austria's ruler during Mozart's early career.

Otto Eric Deutsch, *Mozart: A Documentary Biography*. Stanford, CA: Stanford University Press, 1966. Not only Mozart's letters (less easy to locate than in the Emily Anderson collection) but also reviews, newspaper notices, court documents, and other materials not available elsewhere in English.

Alfred Einstein, *Mozart: His Character/His Work*. New York: Oxford University Press, 1945. A standard text, more authoritative on the music than on biographical data. Intended for the advanced student.

C. G. Girdlestone, *Mozart and His Piano Concertos*. Norman: University of Oklahoma Press, 1952. Reprint of a British work; splendid insights into all of the concertos. For music lovers generally and maturing piano students in particular.

W. H. Hadow, *The Oxford History of Music*, Volume IV. New York: Cooper Square Publishers, 1973. A standard reference work for music and musicians of Mozart's era.

Donald Heartz, *Mozart's Operas*. Berkeley, CA: University of California Press, 1990. A collection of current or earlier essays, with additional material by Thomas Bauman, covering such specialized topics as the theme of human sacrifice in *Idomeneo*, and the role of Donna Elvira in *Don Giovanni*. Intended for advanced students.

Spike Hughes, *Famous Mozart Operas*. New York: Dover Publications, 1972. An inexpensive paperback that takes the reader through scores and librettos with more than three hundred musical excerpts; for anyone who can plunk the piano or sing. Not all of the interpretations are reliable, however.

Dyneley Hussey, *Wolfgang Amade Mozart*. New York: Harper and Brothers, 1928. A fine example of older Mozart scholarship for the general reader, with very sensible evaluations of the composer's major works.

Otto Jahn, *Life of Mozart*. New York: Cooper Square Publishers. 1970. The great nineteenth-century biography in three volumes; still an excellent source for primary materials.

H. C. Robbins Landon, *Mozart and the Masons*. New York: Schirmer Books, 1982. A specialized monograph covering the beliefs, membership lists, and struggles of Viennese Freemason lodges in the 1780s. Not for casual reading.

Paul Henry Lang, editor, *The Creative World of Mozart*. New York: W. W. Norton, 1941, 1963. Musicological studies by specialists of aspects of Mozart's art. Chapter headings indicate subjects covered, such as "Mozartean Modulations," "Mozart and Haydn," and so forth. For advanced students.

Kurt Frank Reinhardt, *Germany: 2000 Years*. New York: F. Ungar and Company, 1961. Political and social history of the German-speaking peoples for those curious about the broader context of Mozart's career.

John E. Rodes, *Germany: A History*. New York: Holt, Rinehart, and Winston, 1964. Another good general history, somewhat more compact than Reinhardt's.

Charles Rosen, *The Classical Style*. New York: W. W. Norton, 1972. Technical analysis of Haydn's, Mozart's, and Beethoven's contributions to the European classical tradition from 1770 to 1830. Numerous musical quotations. For readers with a good knowledge of music theory.

Stanley Sadie, *The New Grove Mozart*. New York: W. W. Norton, 1982. Encyclopedic approach to the career and music, including a definitive list of compositions by date, genre, K. number, and so forth.

Erich Schenk, *Mozart and His Time*. New York: Alfred A. Knopf, 1959. Fine and detailed treatment of biography; less emphasis on the music.

Gary Schmidgall, *Literature as Opera*. New York: Oxford University Press, 1977. As the title suggests, the approach to Mozart and other composers is literary rather than musical.

Peter Shaffer, *Amadeus*. New York: Samuel French, 1980. The stage play from which the film script was adapted. Fine drama, unreliable history.

Patrick J. Smith, *The Tenth Muse: A Historical Study of the Opera Libretto*. New York: Schirmer Books, 1970. Comparable to the Schmidgall title, and an equally perceptive review of operatic texts from the Renaissance to our times, without particular emphasis on Mozart.

Andrew Steptoe, *The Mozart–Da Ponte Operas*. Oxford, England: The Clarendon Press, 1988. A top-notch example of current scholarship, including all kinds of information about *Figaro*, *Don Giovanni*, and *Cosi*. For advanced students.

A Final Note:

Schirmer, Boosey and Hawkes, and others have issued piano-vocal reductions of the major operas with bilingual librettos. *Mozart's Librettos*, translated by Robert Park and Marjorie Lelash (World Publishing Company, Cleveland: 1961), prints bilingual texts on facing pages without the music. The translations are lively but not literal. Individual volumes of librettos with commentaries and illustrations appear in the excellent *English National Opera Series* (John Calder, London: 1970s and 80s). Full orchestral scores with librettos in the original language only, and commentary in German, can be found in separate volumes of *Wolfgang Amadeus Mozart; Neue Ausgabe Samtlicher Werke*, which only large libraries or specialized music libraries would be likely to own. Various editions of the sonatas and other small works, and also miniature scores, are available in smaller libraries and good music stores.

Long-playing and digital albums abound. New performances or rerecordings constantly appear on CDs or tapes. The situation is too fluid for accurate coverage here. Ingmar Bergman's very imaginative *Magic Flute* sung in Swedish is available on video cassette. Don't miss it!

Index

The Abduction from the Seraglio, 40–41, 43, 46, 48–49, 52–53, 58
   plot of, 48
Alceste (Gluck opera), 46
Amadeus (film), 11, 14, 41, 90, 96
Anderson, Emily, 14, 25, 32, 36, 41, 48, 50, 53, 71, 72, 74, 85
Andrade, Francisco d', 96
Arco, Count, 47–48
Ascanio in Alba
   short opera by Mozart, 28–29, 40

Bach, Johann Christian, 22
Bach, Johann Sebastian, 22, 73–74, 87
The Barber of Seville, 59
Barth, Karl, 99
Beaumarchais, Pierre-Augustin, 28, 58–59, 61
Beethoven, Ludwig van, 16, 22, 38, 44, 94–96
   Diabelli Variations, 65
   Fidelio (opera), 76
   first meeting with Mozart, 65
   Missa Solemnis, 87
   opinion about Mozart, 54
   Pastorale Symphony, 72
   prudishness of, 76
Bernstein, Leonard, 96
Bertati (poet), 66
Boccherini, Luigi, 38
Bondini, Pasquale, 64
Brahms, Johannes, 54, 96
   German Requiem, 87
Braunbehrens, Volkmar, 88
Bullinger, Joseph, 33

Canal, Giovanni (Canaletto), 47
Canaletto (Giovanni Canal), 47
Cannabich (Mannheim conductor), 34
Cannabich, Rosa, 34
Carr, Francis, 90
Carrogis, Louis (de Carmontelle), 23
The Clemency of Titus (Metastasio), 78–79
Clementi, Muzio, 52
Colloredo, Prince-Archbishop, 30–31, 33, 44
concertos of Mozart, 53–54, 62, 73
   Coronation Concerto, 75
Conti, Prince, 21

Coronation Concerto (Mozart), 75
Coronation Mass (Mozart), 33
Cosi fan Tutte, 42, 58, 75–78
   plot of, 76
Crankshaw, Edward, 39
Croce, J. N. della, 20

Da Ponte, Lorenzo, 58–61, 66, 70, 75, 78, 86, 94
Dent, Edward J., 89
Deutsch, Otto Eric, 13, 19, 56
Diabelli Variations (Beethoven), 65
Dickens, Charles, 79
Dickinson, Emily, 99
Disodent quartet (Mozart), 57
Dittersdorf (composer), 57, 61
Don Giovanni, 12, 43–44, 58, 64–70

Einstein, Alfred, 45
elegy for a pet bird, 13
Esterhazys (Austrian noblemen), 38
"Exultate Jubilate"
   vocal piece by Mozart, 31

Faust (Goethe), 43
Ferdinand, ruler of Milan, 39
Fidelio (Beethoven), 76
Franklin, Benjamin, 38
Freemasonry (Masons), 15–16, 40, 42, 55, 88–90
Furtwängler, Gustav, 96

George III, king of England, 22
German Requiem (Brahms), 87
Gieseke, Karl Ludwig, 80
Girdlestone, C. W., 97
Gluck, Christoph Willibald, 27–28, 38, 46, 68
G Minor Symphony (Mozart), 12
Goethe, Johann Wolfgang von, 43, 68, 83
Goldoni, Carlo, 28
Göring, Hermann, 99
grand opera (opera seria), 27

Hadow, W. H., 42
Haibl, Sophie Weber, 88, 92–93
Handel, George Frideric, 74
Hasse, Johann, 24, 27
Haydn, Franz Josef, 11, 16, 23, 38–39, 44, 55–57, 96
   his opinion of Mozart, 63
   Mozart's opinion of, 53, 56
   as musical innovator, 43

Hitler, Adolf, 99
Hoffman, E. T. A., 95
Hussey, Dyneley, 95

idiot savant, 12
Idomeneo (Mozart opera), 12, 44–47

Jommelli, Niccolò, 27
Jonson, Ben, 93
Joseph II, emperor of Austria, 39–43, 48, 68, 75–76, 89, 91
Jupiter Symphony (Mozart), 72, 98

Karl Theodore, duke of Mannheim, 44, 46
Kaunitz, Austrian prince, 39
Kelly, Michael, 13
Kennedy, John F.
   conflicts about death of, 90
Kierkegaard, Soren, 95
Köchel (K.)
   directory of Mozart's works, 29
Kozeluch (composer), 53

Lange, Aloysia Weber, 14, 34–35, 37
Lange, Joseph, 37
Leopold II, emperor of Austria, 75, 78
The Letters of Mozart and His Family (Anderson), 25, 32, 36, 41, 50, 72
The Liar (Goldoni), 28
Lichnowsky, Prince, 74
Louis XV, king of France, 20
Lucio Silla (Mozart opera), 29–30

The Magic Flute, 13, 22, 78–84, 94
   plot of, 80–82
Maria Theresa (Crankshaw), 39
Maria Theresa, empress of Austria, 20, 28, 39–40
Marie Antoinette, princess of Austria, 20
The Marriage of Figaro, 13, 30, 58–62, 64
   plot of, 59–60
Martin (composer), 61
Martini, Padre, 25
Masons (Freemasonry), 15–16, 40, 42, 55, 88–90
Mendelssohn, Felix, 94
Metastasio, Pietro, 28, 78
Missa Solemnis (Beethoven), 87

Mitradate (Mozart opera), 25, 27, 30, 40
Molière, 66
Molina, Tirso de, 66
Mozart, Constanza Weber (wife of Mozart), 16, 35, 49–51, 60, 63–65, 67
  concert to aid her, 16
  expressions of love from Mozart, 74–75, 85
  her health, 69, 71, 79
  Mozart's death and, 91
  wrote first biography, 91
Mozart, Franz Xaver (son of Mozart), 51, 84
Mozart, Karl Thomas (son of Mozart), 51, 54
Mozart, Leopold (father of Mozart), 17, 28, 31, 44
  concern about Mozart's lovelife, 34–35
  correspondence with Mozart, 14, 26
  decline and death, 65–66
  Mozart's early education and, 19
  musical training of Mozart, 23–24
Mozart, Maria Anna (Nannerl; sister of Mozart), 17–18, 21–23, 26, 49, 54–55, 66
Mozart, Maria Anna Pertl (mother of Mozart), 17, 32, 34–35
Mozart, Maria Anna Thekla (Bäsle; cousin of Mozart), 35–37
Mozart, Wolfgang Amadeus
  advice on wife's health, 71
  amorous activities, 34–37
  Beethoven and
    first meeting with, 65
    his opinion of Mozart, 54
  as child prodigy, 20–26
  chronology of life and times, 8–9
  death from unknown cause, 87–88
  early education, 19
  early illness, 22
  elegy for a pet bird, 13
  funeral, confusion about, 91
  Haydn and
    Mozart's opinion of, 53, 56
    opinion of Mozart, 63
  as musical innovator, 43
  naughty letter, 36
  physical abuse by Count Arco, 47–48
  pictured, 11, 12, 20, 23, 26, 94
  possible murder of, 88–90
  on public's musical taste, 74, 75
  works of
    concertos, 53–54, 62, 73
      Coronation Concerto, 75
    operas
      The Abduction from the Seraglio, 40–41, 43, 46, 48–49, 52–53, 58
      Ascanio in Alba, 28–29, 40
      Cosi fan Tutte, 42, 58
      Don Giovanni, 12, 43–44, 58, 64–65
      Idomeneo, 12, 43–47
      Lucio Silla, 29–30
      The Magic Flute, 13, 22, 78–84, 94
      The Marriage of Figaro, 13, 30, 58–62, 64
      Mitradate, 25, 27, 30, 40
    other works by
      Coronation Mass, 33
      "Exultate Jubilate," 31
      Requiem, 16, 74, 85–87, 90, 92–93
      Sinfonia Concertante, 33
    quartets
      the Disodent, 57
    quintets, 73
    symphonies, 72
      G Minor, 12
      the *Jupiter,* 72, 98
      the *Prague,* 64
Mozart (Ottaway), 70
Mozart: A Documentary Biography (Deutsch), 13, 16
Mozart and Constanza (Carr), 90
Mozart and His Piano Concertos (Girdlestone), 97
Mozart and His Times (Schenk), 86
Mozarteum, 55
Mozart: His Character/His Work (Einstein), 45
Mozart in Vienna (Braunbehrens), 88
Mozart's Operas (Dent), 89
Mozart: The Man and His Works (Turner), 24, 30, 61, 69, 95

National Theater (Mannheim), 34
The New Grove Mozart (Sadie), 68–69
Nissen, Georg, 50, 91

Olliver, M. B., 21
opera seria (grand opera), 27
Order of the Golden Spur, 25–26
Orpheus and Eurydice (opera by Gluck), 46
Orres, Abbé, 24
Ottaway, Hugh, 70, 96
The Oxford History of Music, 42

Paisiello, Giovanni, 27, 59
Pastorale Symphony (Beethoven), 72
Paumgartner, Bernard, 29
Prague Symphony (Mozart), 64
Puchberg, Michael, 69, 71
Pushkin, Aleksandr Sergeyevich, 96

Raaff, Anton, 44
The Rascal of Seville (Molina), 66
Reinhardt, Kurt Frank, 43
Requiem (Mozart), 16, 74, 85–87, 90, 92–93
Rigoletto (Verdi), 94
The Robbers (Schiller), 43

Sadie, Stanley, 68–69
Salieri, Antonio, 27, 75, 84, 89–90, 96
Salzburg Festival (1960), 29
Schachtner, Johann, 18
Schenk, Erich, 86
Schikaneder, Emanuel, 78–84, 89
Schiller, Friedrich von, 43
Schrattenbach, archbishop of Salzburg, 23
Schubert, Franz, 94
The Servant of Two Masters opera by Goldoni, 28
Shakespeare, William, 79, 93
Shaw, George Bernard, 96
Sinfonia Concertante (Mozart), 33
Singspiel, 28
Solti, Sir George, 96
Sonnenburg, Baron von, 66
Stephanie (poet), 48
Sturm und Drang, 43
Süssmayr (assistant to Mozart), 78, 86–92
Swieten, Baron van, 39, 52, 72, 91

Toscanini, Arturo, 96
Tristram Shandy (Sterne), 37
Turner, W. J., 24, 30, 61, 69, 95

Vanhal (composer), 57
Varesco (librettist), 44, 46
Verdi, Giuseppe, 94
Voltaire, 37

Wagner, Richard, 16, 94, 96
Walsegg, Count, 84
Wren, Sir Christopher, 93

Picture Credits

Cover photo by Historical Pictures/Stock Montage

Archiv für Kunst und Geschichte, Berlin, 12 (top), 18 (both), 20, 21 (both), 22, 26, 27, 29, 30, 33, 34, 35, 36, 37, 39, 40, 43, 44, 45, 46 (both), 47, 50, 51, 52, 57 (bottom), 59, 60, 64, 65, 66, 67, 68, 70, 77, 78, 79, 80, 81, 82, 84, 85, 87, 88, 89, 91, 92, 96, 98

Historical Pictures/Stock Montage, 28, 54, 56, 58, 90

Interfoto Archiv, 23, 57 (top), 75, 76

Internationale Stiftung Mozarteum, Salzburg, 12 (bottom), 55

© Keystone/The Image Works, 17, 24, 97

Library of Congress, 11, 94

Museen der Stadt Wien, 15

Northwind Picture Archives, 38, 49

Acknowledgments

The following publishers have generously given permission to use extended quotations from copyrighted works: Reprinted from *Mozart: A Documentary Biography,* by Otto Erich Deutsch, translated by Eric Blom, Peter Branscombe, and Jeremy Noble, with the permission of the publishers, Stanford University Press and A. and C. Black. Copyright © 1965 by A. and C. Black Ltd. Excerpts from *The Letters of Mozart and His Family* by Emily Anderson are reprinted by permission of W. W. Norton & Company, Inc. Copyright © 1985 by Emily Anderson.

About the Author

Upon graduating from Macalester College in St. Paul, Minnesota-born Roger Blakely went directly into the armed forces, serving as cryptographer at Air Corps bases in Kansas, India, and the Western Pacific from 1943 through 1945. Following advanced study at the University of Minnesota, he joined the faculty of his alma mater to teach English, Art History, and the Humanities until his partial retirement in 1992. His specialties are American writers and interdisciplinary approaches to literature, music, and the visual arts.

He has published one book of mixed prose and poetry about his native state as well as articles on authors Sinclair Lewis and James Wright. He has also co-edited three anthologies of Upper Midwest poems and short fiction.

Music has been a serious pursuit ever since his years in high school and college concert bands. Even more than Beethoven or Schubert, Mozart remains his favorite composer, and he hopes the present volume reflects some of this enthusiasm.